Graffiti Stories

Nick Gerrard

Published By
Breaking Rules Publishing

Soft Cover – 10522
Published by Breaking Rules Publishing
Pompano Beach, Florida
www.breakingrulespublishing.com

Thanks to my two lovely editors

Helen Baggott
Sonya Lano
Cover art by Michal Mráz
Cover design Jana Musilová

Contents

Graffiti

I was born by the side of a walking freak-show
under neon signs shadowed by hookers' arses
and engineers' hammers
In foul-smelling alleys I suckled from a fake tit-
bottle
next to wasted military men
with long beards who drank the long track
pushing shopping trolleys with their lives all in
And this city was my playground
The neighbourhood squabbles my entertainment
The slaps and hair-pulling my action movie
The lady blooded and laddered in the gutter my
horror fest
I tread these streets
I touch the peeling walls, the clattering pipes, the
rotting toilet stench
I pump the heartbeat of the sidewalks
The soul of the folks
The brat machines cluttering the stoops
The vendors pushing their wares

The dealers selling escape
The bottle offering a blur
The vomit glittering in rain drain
The filth of life washing down rusting vents
I know and die with these streets
just a little
day in day
I feel all these hurts
All the pains and belly aches
All the sweat of disappointment
All the drowning of dreams
in a sea of facades
I stand and scream
along-side a mother
taking a selfie
at the feet
of another gang statistic
I drag my sorry arse through the garbage to work
with the boys
on a site of construction
for better places
But not for us

The Queen of Barrio Alto

I always knew where to find him.

Behind Liberty Avenue; full of luxury shoe shops and dear cafés with tree-topped, shaded terraces.

In the scruffy narrow cobbled streets, where people live and work.

There's José's bar and grill, a neighbourhood bar: a few Formica tables, faded Benfica team pictures, and a fuzzy TV.

Full of broken men and a broken grill.

John would be there, you could always find him, though he went there not to be found.

He went there to drink, in between classes, at the posh school on the Avenue.

No one could tell he drank.

He never looked drunk.

Or more to the point he was never sober, so no one knew.

Except me.

And what did I care?

I drank too.

We had met when we had both been living in a flat share, run with an iron fist by the mad Angolan woman, and the travel writer.

She thought everyone was planning to seduce her, and threw fits all the time, and shoes at the writer. She dreamt up drama, it kept her life interesting, but made everyone else's a bit more miserable.

The writer wrote reviews for guide books, but he never visited the bars he reviewed, he got his information from me and John.

The Rough Guide never accepted our submissions.

It was a tall faded beauty of a building, and the flat share took up a whole floor. There were jutting out tight corners, and shuttered doors to unknown little hideaways.

I often bumped into people in the labyrinth of corridors, and greeted them as long lost friends or we introduced ourselves as new ones.

I knew John lived there but I didn't know him. We met sometimes in the kitchen, when I was cooking and he was searching for bottles in the fridge. We would grunt or nod, as one or both of us were usually hung over. And we knew that we should probably stay away from each other for as long as we could.

But inevitably one day we came together and became friends.

I had been flirting with a woman named Xana for a while.

We had met at the cool flat, in the coolest Barrio, of a cool musician, who I disliked as he wasn't cool, just a good actor.

He had invited my friend Vicky to the party. She was a single mum and a great jazz and blues singer.

She had played and got raving drunk with the cool musician, and other musicians.

I often babysat her kid Molly; or took her to the Indian place, so I could drink while I babysat, as the waiters loved her, and entertained her, while I drank and ate lentils.

Vicky and me had also played some small clubs, dueting to my battered acoustic. I even wrote some tunes for her, and we were good.

So, I was kind of invited by proxy and a reputation; for wildness as much as my musicianship. At the party I was fine. There were many would-be bohemians of the Lisbon night.

And I drank but remained witty, and friendly. Xana was the cool musician's girl, but I could tell she was interested in me, by her glances and touches as she squeezed past me.

And god, was she sexy, and flirtatious. A tight blue dress, and wild uncontrollable hair to her shoulders.

Full, pouting lips, that gave a hint of the conquests of her grandfathers, in far-off lands. And the more she drank, the more she danced, the sexier, and less of the cool musician's trophy, she became. I knew we would meet again. It was just a matter of time. The cool musician was frowning.

I had shared a really expensive apartment with two American women, who never went out and dreamed of getting laid by a prince, but baked cookies instead. And I got thrown out for bringing the police there too many times, and setting my shoes alight; burning the ancient wooden floor was the last straw.

So I moved in with the Angolan woman and the guide writer. The rent was low, and I made it by selling photos my Scottish drinking partner and would-be entrepreneur had commissioned some guy to take for us. And he got me making frames and standing in the thieves market for hours. Or we went down to Cascais to get the tourists. And again, our partnership was uneven, as he never seemed to be around for the hours I spent standing next to bloody jugglers and hair braiders. I got my own

back; every time I sold a picture, I retired to a
bar opposite my patch.

After a few weeks of living in the flat and
selling photos, and drinking cheap wine and
eating poor man's soup, I got lonely, lonely for a
woman. I thought of Xana, as she was always
there in the back of my mind, itching me.

So, I did some tracking and rang her, with
the pretence of wanting to talk to the cool
musician, luckily for me she didn't know where
he was. I made my move.

We went dancing in Barrio Alto and
eventually ended up in the bar called *A Kick in
the Cunt*, a real bar, run by this worldly wise old
groupie, who still wore leathers and red lipstick.
And for those who dared there was a drink
called *A Kick in the Cunt*.

And when you drank it everyone
watched, and the withered groupie looked on
with a smirk. Now, I don't know what a kick in
the cunt feels like, but if it's anything like the
drink, then it's bad!

I managed to get Xana back to my room.
She was so kicked. I didn't fuck her.

She wanted to, but I thought I would wait,
so she could remember.

In the morning, the sun shone in through
the bay windows burning into my skull. The

noise of a living street tormented me. I peeled the sheet from around me and looked for something clean to put on, and where the fuck was Xana?

I found her in the living room, slugging back cold beers with John and his even fatter mate Gary from northern England, who was visiting for the summer. Xana was laughing her head off at the boys' talk, and flirting with them like mad. She looked OK, considering the Kicks in the Cunt she had drunk. Very French bohemian chic.

This was Xana's introduction to the *morning beer*, which looking back now, may have been the start of her downfall. I pulled up a stool and poured a glass. Cheers!

We started to feel well, and then better, then good. We went for more beer. The streets were too hot and too busy. I bought a lot of beer, and some bread and crisps, because man cannot live on beer alone. Oh, and loads of fags.

We drank and danced to music that made the people next door and above and below bang, but we didn't care. We danced on the small balconies, in our underpants. Danced to all the top gay tunes, and shouted sexual innuendoes, and wolf whistled. And the classic *Look at meat on that!* said in a mock northern accent, I don't know, somewhere between Blackburn and Bury. I joined in and camped it up with the two Queens.

The two Queens, were the least 'gay' gay guys I had ever met.

They were flabby from beer, their hair was not groomed, in fact greasy from alcohol sweats, as was their skin, their teeth were bad and they had bad dress sense, well not bad, they just didn't care.

There were no flat tummies, the only six packs they...you get the picture!

No pecs but man tits. No manicured fingers but yellowy nibbled nails.

There was nothing obviously gay about them, apart from their outrageous campiness, which made me howl, and confused and scared the ordinary man to death.

Xana and I decided now was a good time to fuck, before we got too drunk; we did, we slept. We woke up to a clock ringing, which I threw out the window. I picked Xana off my legs and tried to figure out the time, the day. Shit, the clock was gone. It was dark. We dressed as best we could and went into the living room, to find the two Queens still drinking in their underpants. We both went to the toilet to retch then we sat down to drink. They decided we needed a change in scenery. So gathering ourselves and throwing bits of clothes on as best we could, and holding each other up along the streets, we made it to the chicken piri-piri joint a block or two away. We ate and switched to wine, we felt better and got well, and felt good enough to finally, after a few hours, retire to sleep again. Life in the apartment kind of went on like this, never ending and intense, like the summer sun.

I would wake up, walk into the living room, and the guys would be there, in shorts or pants; always a beer in hand, laughing or singing.

It was no bender because they never stopped.They would drink at home all day then go on fag crawls all night.

Sometimes they left, in taxis of course, hammered, and would return three days later to resume their positions near the balcony.

Re-telling tales of the guys they'd blown, or fucked or fought. I was amazed that these drunken road-menders from the North, could get laid. They were the opposite of everything that is classed as classy gay; rude, obnoxious, fat, ugly, smelly, drunks.

But I think they were attractive to gay guys because of this very thing. They were the 'fuck it' guys. More manly than a stevedore, filthier than a rent boy on dope, more drunk than a can-factory alley cat.

And I loved those guys.

I loved the whole anarchic drama of them.

I thought I was a good 'fuck it' guy, but these guys, these guys, were the queens of *Fuck it!*

They invited me out one night on a fag crawl. I was honoured.

All the crawling was done in taxis, they had a bit of class.

Shit, I was wasted before we even left the apartment. I struggled to get in the taxi, and when we pulled up outside this little corner, with fags hanging out, outside little bars and cafés, in narrow streets, like in some Mexican border town, I pulled the door handle off as I fell out the cab. A big argument ensued as I tried to get my legs to stand my body up. The taxi driver was screaming and the bouncers from a little doorway came over and the street looked on, as tinny dance music laid the backing track. The driver was sent on his way, with a bloody nose and some cash, and a warning. The Queens knew everybody. They kissed eager lips, slapped friendly hands. It was like royalty were visiting. I was helped into a café by their followers, and dosed up in the toilets.

I came out, refreshed and able to stand, I
was given drinks, and my head started to clear
and I began to feel good, really good.

I was riding a wave. We surfed from bar
to café, to club. Everyone encouraging us on.
We were the champions!

I was the bar king of Lisbon. I could find
you a Cape Verdian house that served you fried
chicken and beer at 4am on a Tuesday morning,
but the Queens knew places I hadn't even heard
of. As they walked along a street, it seemed like
places would open up, just for them.

We were ushered into clubs, quickly
given tokes, and passed E's like Smarties. To
keep us going, everyone wanted us to keep
going, urging us on. Even the police seemed to
be on their side when they needed them.

We were in a half fag, half straight club,
and a female friend of mine was being hassled by
this would-be macho guy, she came over and
asked me to help. I went and remonstrated with
the guy, and his mates. He got all aggressive and
pushy, and shouty, and Gary walked over and
head-butted him. The guy's nose cracked open.
The bouncers stopped any further bloodshed by
kicking the man with the bent nose and his
chums out.

But then there was trouble at the door, a

larger gang of guys now, were, pushing and shouting with the bouncers as they tried to enter on mass to get at us.

'Fuck this!'

'We can't wait in here all night.'

'Are you ready?'

I wasn't but shit, when your mates go, you go!

They got to the door and stripped off their tops, and pushed their way into the middle of the group, with me shitting myself beside them.

The magnificent three! The gang's gung-ho was shattered a little by our bravado. A few kicks rained in, and we punched and butted.

We fought as we backed up the streets of Barrio Alto, cheered on by workmen up scaffolds and prostitutes on balconies.

It seemed that word had spread and the gang grew in number. We picked up handy wooden poles to help. The mayhem was halted by a group of guys, I didn't know who they were, but they held us and the gang members apart. Insults and threats were now rained in on us as all. We laughed in faces, and now and again smacked one or two with our poles.

It became clear that the guys holding the trouble back were cops. And despite the protests of the Pork and Cheese would-be hooligans, we were escorted out of the Barrio, and seen safely into our preferred mode of transport. And as we squeezed up in the back, panting and buzzing and laughing our heads off, in relief, and filled with adrenalin; we flicked the finger at the frustrated remonstrating mob, and flew away with a screech of tyres, and whizzed hastily chopped lines of Charlie up our noses.

After a couple of months, I had an offer of a better room, in a saner apartment and Gary moved in full-time to my room. Seemed like he couldn't leave; he was on the bender to end all benders.

I didn't see the guys that often, we drank in different circles, but our paths would inevitably cross from time to time, and drugs were shared and stories told and beers sank, as we laughed and laughed, and hugged, at some crowded bar of a café, or trendy club.

One Sunday afternoon I was walking home alone, after a long night that had become breakfast and lunch. And feeling in need of a change of clothes and some sleep. I had reluctantly left some friends who went to enjoy a day at the beach. I walked slowly, easing my pains with shots of Ginjinha, in the little stand up bars, on the backstreet, near Rossio, where they squeeze in between the restaurants with spider crabs in the window. Near the end of the street, there was a small café, with a fairly large group of chatting and happy guys spilling out into the street.

I thought it only polite to have a drink there. As I pushed through the throng, there was Gary and John, at the bar, holding court.

After kisses and hugs, and toasts, above the din, John told me that this was the usual meet-up place for the hard-core gay guys, on a Sunday, where they came down gradually from the weekend's adventures. I was coming up again, never mind coming down.

'Yeah, here and next door of course!'

'Next door?'

John laughed and led me by the hand through the twitching giddy mass.

Next door, I stopped to look up.

It was an old art deco building, with a small but elegant entrance of columns.

It was now a porno cinema.

'A porno cinema, you're kidding right?'

John flung his head back with his guttural laugh.

'Come on, Mr bloody naive!'

And grabbing me by the hand we entered.

The inside of the foyer resembled a seedy

Arabic harem. There were red and black drapes flowing down, and armchairs all around. The smoke sat mid-air, adding to the whole haze of the place. Every chair was occupied by gay guys of all sizes and ages and occupation. Young guys sat on the chair arms of fat loud-shirted older guys. Some looked like English

Lords and smoked with holders.

I was starting to stop feeling well. And after a quick beer was downed, I made a dash for the toilets. In the ceramic tiled loos, various wellness therapies were being administered. From squeals of pleasure from a cubicle, to the chop-chopping on the sink tops, in front of the ornate mirrors, underneath the golden lamps. I was handed a sliver tube, and welcomed to bend over. I was well again.

I returned to the foyer, and got drunk, and returned to the pleasure toilets when I needed to, and sometimes just because I wanted to. I never paid for anything. I was John's guest, and guests of the Queen were well looked after.

John whispered in my ear, 'You should try the theatre.'

'Cheers, man. But you know, gay films, not really my thing!'

'Do you think they would let us watch gay porn in here?'

Well, with what the hell else was going on, I thought a few films wouldn't really be pushing the boundaries of acceptable behaviour.

I walked into the auditorium, and in the hazy lights I sat and watched heterosexual porn films.

And a blow job is a blow job, and 100 escudos is, well, a bargain!

I loved that cinema, and popped in again when I was at a loose end, on a Sunday.

I left Lisbon a few years down the line; the life was too much and it was time to try and stop killing myself.

A few years later I went back, for a holiday, with a woman I liked a lot. I took her for a 'Kick in the Cunt', but she preferred the wine and the clams in the splendour of Casa Alentaju, and the spider crab restaurants rather than the Ginjinha bars. After a long night, she decided she needed half a day in bed.

I thought I would check out some places I couldn't take her.

I passed the posh shops on the Avenue, and found the little streets where people live and work. And entered José's bar and grill. I was happy to see the grill was still not working, but unhappy to see no John sitting on his usual stool at the bar.

I sat on his stool and shook hands with José, happy to not be forgotten.

And John? He wasn't there. José and I raised our beer glasses and toasted him, as he told me John had died.

From a disease that had interfered with his lifestyle and his whole philosophy on how one should live life.

How did he die? Many stories are told. And the one I tell is this:

He could not waste away, that wasn't him.

I heard he walked to Casal Ventosa, where the junkies line up on the hillside by the abandoned buildings, called 'the shooting gallery', where you look out over the beauty of the seven hills. He took a shot. And as the junkies looked on, he climbed half-way down the hillside, and then stripped down to his large stained white Y-fronts. He climbed the pillions of the *Lover's Bridge*; a place famous for the suicide leaps of young lovers.

And with one last 'Fuck it', with an audience of no-hopers, his two fingers raised in a defiant last gesture to convention, he rolled his head back and howled with laughter and shouted:

'Look at the meat on this!'

And leapt.

Norman, Return to Saltley Gate

When I was a younger man, myself and a group of friends lived in south Birmingham.

We shared old rundown Victorian houses, rented out as bedsits.

They were cheap, which is just as well, as we had no paid work as such.

The factories had all been closed down, but we got by on a weekly cheque.

We didn't seem to need much.

And fags, food and booze were shared, whenever someone had them.

We weren't lazy.

We were in fact, busy as hell.

We did courses, and helped out at the Unemployed centre.

Some of us campaigning, others swapping skills, and learning new ones.

We played in bands, we designed posters, we raised money, we protested; we occupied job centre rooves, we rioted.

We bought cheap food from the Asian shops and ate out at balti houses.

We drank and sang rebel songs in the Irish pubs.

And smoked with the Rastas in illegal gambling houses.

We were very political; we lived in political times.

We campaigned for jobs and against job cuts.

We worked with unionised workers and also helped unemployed people get what was theirs.

And we stopped those snooper squads snooping in our areas.

We went on demonstrations against missiles, Irish massacres, fascists, against slave labour schemes.

We bought dope and dealt a little speed, here and there.

We robbed, we drank, we laughed in the sun with the working girls; sat on the huge windowsills listening to dub bass, in the forecourts of those faded brown-brick buildings.

Life was kind of sweet then.

But things started to hot up.

People got pushed more and more to desperation, and more and more into action of one sort or another.

The government forced their economic strategies on an already gasping working class.

Then the big one.

The Great Strike.

She came for war.

She wanted to wipe out our best troops. Then we would all be easier targets.

Suddenly, we were busy, doing what people do in wars.

We collected money from the Asian shop owners, food outside the cheapest supermarkets, and the posh ones.

We got more from people with less.

We were picketing, and battling, and demonstrating.

We sat in miners' social clubs discussing armed revolution with hardened men.

They listened to us, and forgot our weird hair, our skin colour, our sexual preference, our lack of work.

They had thought us, the enemy within.

Now suddenly they were themselves, the enemy within.

So they listened.

And so did we.

We listened to trade unionists who talked like our grandfathers had.

We listened to new/old ideas, new/old politics.

We met people from universities who explained stuff.

And diggers on lines who showed us stuff.

We knew things were wrong, we knew what was not right, we knew how to hate.

We had learned that.

Now these people told us why things were the way they were.

And maybe how we could make things right.

During this time I met a man called Norman.

He had been a leader. A shop steward for the engineers.

He had led out men to block the inland port of Saltly Gate.

In support of the miners some years before, in another battle.

The engineers had won an historic victory.

The guys on the floor had organised themselves despite their boneless leaders.

They had newspapers; they had their organisations within the organisation.

They then had to battle those spineless paid leaders as well.

Now, years later, Norman was jobless.

Sold down the Swanee, by those suited men.

Blacklisted by the bosses and let down by left-leaning groups.

He was a gentle man.

But his fight had not been tampered with.

He had no work, just a disabled wife and kids to care for.

He was thoughtful and simple, and intelligent.

He had learnt from doing, but he also read what needed to be read.

We met often; on demos, in political meetings, in back street pubs.

I liked his views and enthusiasm; his humour and his hospitality.

We went round his modest council house, where we shared crisps and beers, and always watched *Reds*.

But what struck me most about this man was his ability to carry on.

His belief in his beliefs.

When pushed to the bottom of the ruck, this man was still there; on his back, still trying to land a couple of good ones.

I looked up to this man.

And then something happened.

I saw something I had never seen in all the Lefties, all the talkers and activists.

All the angry youth and strikers even.

After the death of the miners.

Other struggles carried on, as they do.

We had been picketing for weeks. The middle of the night, in the draining rain.

We were picketing the newspaper distribution depots.

The printers of the news in London had been sacked.

They and others were trying to stop the delivery of the news.

There was solidarity all over the country.

There had been bitter battles.

There had been deaths.

We met each night in the tower blocks that looked out over the night lights of a hazy Brum.

We drank coffee, wrapped scarves where we could; put plastic bags in our boots.

And then we walked, mostly silently, smoking, through the deserted crisp streets.

We knew the paper handlers well.

And after our usual appeals, arguments, shouting matches, we shared tea and cigs and chatted.

They were sympathetic, but once again some snake had instructed them not to support the Union men.

We sympathised, reluctantly.

Our main purpose was to stop the black-leg lorry drivers, bringing that news from London.

They should not have been bringing it.

They had crossed those lines in London.

And now were doing the same here.

We were seeking solidarity.

One night, we were doing our usual merry dance of push and shove with the police.

I saw out of the corner of my eye, Norman, walking calmly past the crowd.

He approached the stopped truck.

He stepped up to that truck and opened the door.

We all stopped, and watched, and listened.

Norman opened that door and leaned in towards the man, trying to hide behind his wheel.

He pointed a finger at that man; he looked at that man, and with his whole being, his full anger, his whole history...

Cried.

'You're betraying your class, brother.'

The words came from somewhere deep inside.

The very core of his existence.

His whole body tensed and shook.

It was like something primeval.

It wasn't loud; he didn't need to shout.

But it thundered out.

Like a shout from an ancestor's grave.

This was the pleading scream of a slave.

The man started to protest but Norman didn't argue.

He just looked at that man, listened and said again,

'You're betraying your class, brother.'

That man looked for a way out.

For words to defend himself.

But he knew.

He knew and felt this call of the wild.

We could see it had stirred something deep inside him.

Others surrounded this man's truck and hurled insults,

'Scab.'

They argued with him, pleaded with him.

Now this man was able to argue, and

answer back.

But, we who were arguing with this man stopped.

Norman's words came out again.

'You're betraying your class, brother.'

And the man stopped.

The angry youth stopped.

The academic stopped.

The activist stopped.

The warehouse worker stopped.

The police stopped.

I stopped.

And this man started to cry.

And we turned our backs and walked away.

And I watched Norman take this man, and embrace him.

And they spoke no words.

And in each other's arms, Norman patted his back and quietly, into his ear he said,

'I know...I know.'

I had never seen that before.

Never seen anyone express what is just written about.

What is just shouted about.

Or argued about or discussed.

Never seen anyone express their political

views, not just as a theory, but as an actual living part of themselves.

An essential part of their very existence.
And that man turned his truck around.
And without a cheer or a whisper.
He took that news back to London.

Freaks

Big Graham lived in a tree for a while.
That was the story, well that was one of the many
stories that went around about him. And that
one was true. It was a big tree. I mean you could
get inside it. You could climb up and get inside it
and live in it. Big Graham lived there for a year
or so until he decided it was time for a change.
He enjoyed the freedom, the lack of
commitment and, of course, the fresh air.

He didn't care about his toilet, easily dealt
with, and washing never bothered him. He had a
girlfriend. I say girlfriend but Pauline was no
girlfriend; someone to shag and enjoy life with.
Pauline never washed either, why would she?
She had Graham.

I first met Graham at an open-air party in
a garden of a forgotten five-storey house on the
Pershore Road that leads out of Brum. There
was a big fire of scrap furniture and chopped
trees. People stood around it passing spliffs and

wise words, sipping cans of red-stripe, grooving to the heavy dub booming out from massive speakers. Graham, and some shorter scruffy imps, drove a battered old Ford van right through the garden and screeched to a halt by the fire. They bundled out Keystone Cop fashion and dumped out a huge safe before the watching flocks.

"So, anyone know how to break into this thing?"

"What is it?"

"What is it? What is it? It's a fooking safe, mannnn."

Graham stomped round the fire, singing. "It's a fooking safe, it's a fooking safe. We've stolen ourselves a safe, a big fuck off safe. Now all we have to do is open the bigggg fookin' safe."

Hammers were tried, and axes.

"Fuck it! Let's burn it. Burn the fooking safe. Burn the fooking safe ... eee-iii ... the paddy eye we're burning the fooking safe."

Steve arrived with Rat; one straight with a tash, the other punk with a Mohican.

Both thieves and sometimes pimps.

"What the fook you doing, man?"

"Trying to burn the safe."

He laughed.

"Grah, roll that fooker off the fire man."

Steve dipped into his inside pocket, took out a pouch of implements and did what he does best.

We were disappointed, such a big safe but it held little. A couple of hundred quid, some important looking papers and a couple a blocks of black, and a bag of Black and Whites.

Graham burnt the papers and shared the rest out. It was a party.

And that was Graham, never one for possessions, generous with all he had, would give you his last toke if you needed to take it.

The pills kicked in and the party kicked off, then we ran out of booze.

Graham organized a break-in at the offy up the road. A steady stream of soap-spike-haired punks and moustached casuals formed a chain to carry crates down the Pershore Road.

That was my first meeting with Graham, but not my last. He was always around the underground of Brum, whatever was going on, from gigs to fighting the fash, squatting to stealing.

I saw him on the bus one day, the number one from Moseley, he was chatting away to all and sundry; me, old ladies, tramps, and workers, as a little punkette went down on him. He never missed a beat. She finished and he stood and danced and banged his head on the ceiling, and leaped off before the bus came to a halt, like a ballet dancer. He took a bow, we all applauded.

Once, skinheads were beating little punks at a Joke gig at Digbeth town hall. Into the gap walked Graham, he calmly took off his padlock and chain from around his neck, smiled, raised his hand in front of him and beckoned the watching skins coming towards him. After he dusted himself down he leapt around. A war dance!

The Teds in the centre were smacking any stray New Wave kids who hung out at Oasis, checking for reduced bondage trousers, and Reddigtons rare records for any possible releases. It got so bad that kids were afraid to walk around town. Graham and Pauline bounced over to the Turks Head, alone, hand in hand, singing and laughing. I watched from across the road as bodies came hurtling through windows, and quiffed ones tried to escape but got pulled back in by their drainpipes.

Graham and Pauline came out arm in arm, laughing and skipping, swapping blood and spit and laughs from lip to lip.

Pauline was beautiful. The wildest wild woman a man could dream of, over there, alive, a little explosive bundle of grime, sex, sweat and dreadlocks. Every teenage spike tops' kick.

She took shits in bags on buses, and pissed where she stood, and teased and flirted and bigged-up every boy she ever met.

One night in the old porno cinema, while the Drongos played on the heart-shaped red stage, with florescent lighting, she lay back and shoved chocolate bars up her fanny and invited the boys to taste her. Over the years we all travelled more, or moved to other cities.

The underground was large, and friendships wide. We bumped into each other at Blues in Brum, or on Road-menders floors in Northampton. We drank piss together from cider flagons at festivals in Oxford, and then stonked on stage with reggae bands in parks in London town. At political rallies Pauline and Graham led charges with factory men who let their fears and passions go, and they led the hordes against fascists of the blue and of the white persuasion.

For a while Pauline moved into Graham's tree. But that tree was too small, not for their bodies, which fitted nicely. It wasn't big enough in other ways, something to do with their spirits, so Pauline got her own tree.

Nowadays, if you're in Camden Town

sometime, on the off chance, see that stall in the corner? Yeah, that one with the 50s gear and the space suits and bongs. That's Pauline's place. She might not be around, but you might find her drinking in the Elephant, stonking in Dingwalls, or having a spliff and a mug of tea near her counter, her blonde dreadlocks spread all over the floor.

On the South Bank, take your seat in the cool, alternative theatre for the underground French circus. Watch as out of the shadows a huge torso with a tattooed head and raving black eyes man trapezes over the crowd. Say hello to Graham as you jerk back in fear and wonder as he leaps and breathes out a mighty roar of flames over the top of your head.

Safecrackers

Lisa pushes her hands into the mush, squeezing red through her knuckles, trying to find bits that will hold together.

-Hold on, shit, don't fucking move!

-He fucking shot me...can you fucking believe 'e...he fucking shot me...Fuck!

-Don't fucking move then, course it's gonna hurt.

She pushes down hard and holds on.

Across the pub, propped up against the front of the worn oak bar lies a rocker, with a big gash on his head and a knife sticking out of his shoulder, his head is bobbing, and bubbles of spit and blood pop, and dribble from his mouth.

-Is he gonna die?

-I don't think so, but anyway fuck him, I need to keep you alive.

-What about the other one?

-Not sure.

-It hurts like a bitch.

-You'll be alright.

Lisa leans her head on Charlie's, the big clock ticks. A group of revellers are singing 'Dancing Queen' as they weave past the stained windows of the pub.

She makes a call, gets John to pick them up.

She presses a little harder and smiles at Charlie.

He smiles then winces, squeezing some pain out as he tries to get himself comfortable.

-Bet you never expected this when I suggested moving to the city.

They both grin and sniff little laughs.

-You're not fucking kidding.

She bends and kisses his temple.

Charlie and Lisa grew up in a small industrial town, dragged there kicking and screaming in the early seventies from the big city nearby; dragged to grime and soot and nothing to do but work and drink. Work was in factories that made carpets or iron. Drink was upstairs in supporters' club meetings, down the Union halls, round the back alley or behind the park bandstand.

Kids were kept in line with put downs and whacks, and slippers and canes.

That's where they had first met, in a local Working Men's club, a Thursday night disco, mid-seventies Northern soul.

Both fourteen years passing for seventeen, but no one cared, everyone got served.

He spotted her from the bar, her pastel blue soul skirt swirling round. He glimpsed black knickers when she span. Short blonde hair, red lips. He was transfixed.

For the next few weeks he watched her, surrounded by older moustache and vest wearing soul boys; trying to impress her with their moves, their money and their banter. She laughed at their cheesy attempts at chat-up lines, but sometimes snogged them anyway.

He never could get up the nerve to talk to her; she only seemed interested in older blokes. He hated those soul boys with their wide flares and wide lies.

1978

He loved the new sound, the new looks, the do-it-yourself attitude, the *so what!* And the music was short, sharp and powerful. He got some drain-piped trousers from an army surplus store; cut his hair short, spiked it and dyed it black; he already had the boots from the footy. He listened to John Peel play the Lurkers, the Vibrators, 999, and dub.

And then there was the Clash; singing about their lives, and giving two fingers up to it all.

There was nowhere to go, nothing to do. Nothing but falling-to-bits council estates and tired pubs and old-times terraced streets littered with chip papers and pissed up straights.

There were only local soul discos in backstreet dance halls, or upstairs above a pub, for one night only. And sometimes a mate would play the Boomtown Rats, the Skids, The B52s, the Jam, the Ruts, and sometimes even the Pistols or maybe the Damned or some reggae. Fifteen minutes of rebellion out of a night of regular backdrops and spins.

He would get up with four mates and pogo around, fight a bit, skank around a bit, stomp a bit. Just moving, with a passion, with a rage, for fifteen minutes only; the raga and the rage.

And some laughed, but some looked on with interest. And behind the soul girl's giggles, behind the laughing tashes, the red lips and flares, were interested eyes, glancing eyes.

She laffed, but she looked, straight into his eyes. Just for a few seconds, but she looked.

-I like your hair.

He was stood waiting at the bar.

-Thanks. Pint of mild, please.

-You're Charlie Waites aren't you?

-And you're Lisa Stanford, you know me?

-Such a small place, of course I've heard of you.

-Yeah, all good I suppose?

-Not really. *She smiled.* But then I suppose you've only heard bad things about me too?

-I never take stories seriously, they're just stories, mostly bullshit, most of the time.

-Can I get you a drink?

-Thought you'd never ask.

-Rum and black, please.

They sat down and chatted, and made each other laugh, and chatted some more, and sipped and smiled.

-So, you wanna walk me home?

-Love to.

They walked through the red-brick streets. Got chips from a Chinky takeaway, jumped up on a wall. The romantic aroma of beer and Charlie perfume merged with Tobi

Legend's 'Time Will Pass You By' coming through a council house window, he leaned in. And he tasted love; and love tastes of red lipstick and vinegar, No 6 tipped and Bank's mild.

They started courting, meeting up at discos or round friends' houses, with bottles of cider and Ouija boards, and fumbles with bra straps on a single bed; breasts smelling of fresh bread and clean babies' bums. And fingers tight inside each-others pants; fumbling, scratching, scrapping, pushing. Lips and tongues, fags and apple breath.

And the ache inside their chests got stronger, the butterflies in their bellies flapped their wings faster and faster the more they didn't see each other.

They went out, and went babysitting, so they had somewhere private, somewhere to masturbate each other, and try out fucking, which wasn't successful but they wanted to try it, just to kind of get it out of the way. And at the end of the night they had to scrub the sofa and carpet of stains.

One year on

-What the fuck happened?

Lisa sat down in the Wheatsheaf lounge, her eye turning purple and her nose and check scratched.

-He's a fucking arsehole, you know that.

-He did this?

-Yeah.

-What did your mum say?

-My mum got it worse than me, I jumped on his back and smacked him round the face. He was pissed out of his head again, and smacking my mum around the kitchen.

-Fucker!

-He's just a fucking cunt. She's tried to get him out but she always takes him back or he worms his fucking way back in somehow.

-What about the police?

-Yeah, like they are gonna do anything.

-Yeah, well fuck this, I'll fucking get some guys together and we can have a word or two with him.

-No, it would only make things worse for us.

He kissed the purple skin under her eye, she slid her hand down his cheek.

They dreamed of leaving, of escaping, of getting the fuck out. Somewhere else, some-where better, hopefully.

Lisa's stepdad was a fuck-up, a big man about town but a fuck-up all the same. He was a dealer and got high on his own supply. Which was OK apart from the late night parties when he came back with other reprobates for a session. But it was when he on a bender that things got bad. On the gear he was bearable, and Lisa's mum liked a line and a puff and a drink. And sometimes at those times when the mixture was right, when just the right amount of poison was consumed, there was romance and passion between them. Just enough to keep them together, just enough to make the beatings worth it.

But once he'd had too much booze in him, another man came out, a mean, bitter and twisted fucked-up man.

And he hated her mother, hated Lisa too and the boyfriends she saw. And more than all the other hates was the hate he felt for himself, so he beat up those close to him to be able to bear his miserable life.

The two women hid, they kissed and hugged, they escaped. They stole his money when he slept, they kicked him when he was comatose. They scratched him, slapped him, and got punched and kicked and slapped, and hugged and spoilt and fed.

Lisa tried to get her mum to leave, but her mum was afraid, of him, of leaving, of being alone.

But the beatings just carried on, everything just carried on.

Charlie hadn't seen or heard from her for a few days, he was worried. He went round late; he knocked on the door.

-What the fuck do you want?

-Can I speak to Lisa?

-No you can't, now fuck off!

He noticed blood on his hands, he pushed his way in.

-Get the fuck out of my way, you drunken fuck.

-I told you to get the fuck out of here, you little wanker.

He grabbed hold of Charlie's hair and dragged him back, but he slipped.

Charlie got up and started laying into him.

-You mother...fuck...er...I'll fucking teach...you...to...fuc...king!

The fists smashed into his face, again and again, and blood burst from his eyebrows, and his lips bulged blue instantly.

Lisa came down the stairs, with a rounders bat.

Whack!

His skull popped and slammed into the pastel pink wall.

They both stood over the limp man, panting, trying to catch their breaths.

-Is he dead?

Charlie leaned close to his mouth, and among the fumes he felt breath.

-No, but I think we've fucked him up pretty good.

-Not good enough.

Lisa started smashing his arms and legs with the bat, cracking bones.

-Mother...fucking...drunken...fucking...Argh...

She laid into him, all her frustrations, all her anger came out through that bat.

Charlie stopped her after a while and leaned in close to his face again.

-Still not dead.

They went into the kitchen and bathed each other's cuts, made a cuppa and added a splash of whiskey for their nerves.

-We need to leave this place, tonight. How's your mum?

-Battered but OK, she's staying with my

aunt.

-OK, grab what you need, and I'll meet you down town, by the Bay Horse.

They kissed on the doorstep, harder than they had ever kissed before.

-I know where we can get some cash.
-Where?
-The Irish Club, they have a safe.
-Yeah, but do they have any money?
-Probably not much, but it's always full of big drinkers.
-And Punks, would be like stealing from friends.
-Or lending it from friends.

He shrugged and laughed.

-OK, let's do it.

They were sat in a tacky spruced-up Capri, in the Bay Horse car park, in town; a red one with a black stripe down the side.

Charlie had nicked it off the estate, obviously from a *Starsky and Hutch* fan, sad fucker!

-You ready?
-Sure, let's do it.

They got out and walked a couple of blocks, slowly, arm in arm; two lovers on their way home.

It was late and only a few people littered the streets; drunks trying to find their way home, a few groups looking for a lock-in or a late night curry house.

Opposite the indoor market on the corner of the big roundabout stood the three wooden huts that made up the Irish Club, they vaulted the back wall into a little shielded bay area.

They smashed the padlock with a hammer and easily kicked in the flimsy delivery doors.

Through torchlight they made their way to the bar.

-What'll you have?

Lisa pulled up a stool, and grinned.

-Why, kind sir, I'll have a whiskey and ginger, no ice.

-A fine choice, madam, I think I'll join you.

Charlie poured two long ones.

-To new beginnings.

They clinked glasses, drank and leaned heads together over the bar.

-Now, where is this safe?

-You're standing right on it

He pulled back the rubber mat and lifted up a wooden trap door, and there was a small black safe built into a lump of concrete.

-Shit, I thought we could just lift the bloody thing out, then smash it open later.

Lisa smiled, got up and came round the bar. She took out a little case, unzipped it and laid out what looked like dentist tools on the side of the bar.

-Now, I'll show you a few things I picked up from my real dad before he left for good.

-I knew you knew some, but do you think you can handle this?

Lisa stepped up, moved him to the side, and got to work on the lock. Charlie stood on the other side of the bar savouring his drink, smiling and nodding, watching his girl. God she was beautiful! And clever too.

-Voila!

-Shit, you know a lot! How much is there?

-Four or five hundred or so.

-Cool, let's get going.

They grabbed some bottles and crisps and smashed the fag machine, stuffed it all into a duffle bag and slipped out the wooden doors.

They sauntered arm in arm back to the

Capri, and headed for the city.

Early 80s

Life wasn't easy to begin with. There was no work, but the money they had stolen helped them furnish a bedsit in a Victorian house, where they shared a bathroom and toilet with a couple of working girls.

Their rent was paid by the Social and the fortnightly cheques were just enough to get by on. They could eat well with cheap cuts off the rag market on a Saturday afternoon and good veg from the Asian grocers. Most weeks, just enough to scrape by. But some weeks, they had no electric, no booze, and worst of all, no fags.

So naturally they looked for ways to improve their lot, ways to live a decent life.

Cash to enjoy a reasonable life.

Lisa's safecracking skills came in handy. They emptied the gas fire's slot meter in their flat, careful to leave a few fifty pence coins for the landlord. And soon they had a little business going, emptying the meters of the other tenants and friends nearby, for a little fee.

Word got round, and people came calling for the safecrackers' services; people's meters, of course, cheap safes and security boxes that junky cat burglars had stolen. And sometimes they opened the backs of shops late at night.

With the money they earnt they were able to score some weed and a little speed. Go for an Indian or Chinese when stoned. Go to the Fighting Cocks regularly for beer and rock. The Red Lion for blues and weed. Or they got dolled up for a night out in town on acid; all-nighters at a blues with speed and ska, or down the gambling house for bets, red stripe, spliffs, dub and mad-chats.

They always had friends round for food and a smoke.

They started to love their life, love the adventure, the thrill; the music, the drink, the drugs.

Charlie played bass in a Clash-rock-reggae band and Lisa did art courses down the unemployed centre.

They moved into another Victorian house and got two rooms, and their own kitchen and bathroom.

They smiled and rested their heads on each other's, and clinked wine glasses on the steps on a sunny evening, and as the girls worked the streets they kissed as they exhaled smooth smoke slowly from an introverted spliff.

As they got more cash they got more gear, they started dealing a little; a few tablets here, a gram of wiz there, an eighth passed on with only a slice for profit. They never started out with the idea of making money, it was about creating a good feeling. When travelling punks hitched up in town they supplied all the needs; getting cheaper draw from the Jamaicans for bulk buying, and making a little with the pass on. People turned up for the after gig party in the overgrown garden at the back, to fire-dance and rant. To share a floor in sleeping bags, and laughs and snogs, and drugs and hugs.

They loved the friendships they made, the community spirit, the under-class; the hookers and drug pimps, the striking man and Lefty uni prof. The hobo punk and hippie artist, the greasy musician and Rasta toaster.

As is nearly always the case, their own habits increased, their own consumption of hard drugs grew, and with it the mood swings, the bad come-downs, the paranoia, the pain. So grams became ounces, eighths became quarters. And one night awake became two, became four.

And happy smiling friend-filled cool breeze evenings, became dank back-alley staircases and needles in ill-heated bare bedsits. They borrowed gear to sell gear to pay for gear to top themselves up, then the need for more became a need for more, to lend some more to sell some more to need some more.

They reined each other's excesses in, for the sake of each other, for the sake of themselves. They had each other to keep check on each other. They stopped each other crossing the line. There were mood swings, and fights, and arguments over petty shit, and bad come-downs, and lost days. They saw each other through, just about, kept each other back, on the right side of that thin line.

There was a rocker's pub, the Green Man. The gang who ran it were called the Outcasts. A city bikers' gang with few bikes, but they had connections, with the Angels and organized criminals. They dealt in everything, from smack to hash, robbery to gash. They kept the Green Man, a place to hang, a place to organize, a home. Where metal heads gathered to smoke the black man's weed in peace, with cider and napalm death, and mucky blondes with smeared black eyes, denim, and big creamy tits.

The clubs in town didn't really cater to the tastes of the young people, not the inner city kids. They catered to the estate kids, the outer-ring-road kids. There were a few discos where casuals flocked to drink and fight and find a gran to fuck. Dear entrance and disco balls, Dexys and The Specials, aggro and flicks.

There was no venue that catered to the tastes of the inner city crews, nowhere in the centre where they could come together, people from the North- and South-sides. No place that mixed punk with dub, New Wave with ska. It was one or the other, sometimes at parties or one-off gigs.

Charlie and Lisa saw a chance to start something up, to make a few quid as well, but really just for the hell of it. They had a mate who had a job as a security guard, for a few disused warehouses near the post office tower just off the ring-way.

Underneath the old grey-brick ten-storey building was a huge cellar, a labyrinth of small rooms and a couple of large ones. The place was fairly clean and dry.

A group of mates went with Charlie and Lisa to check it out and an idea was born, the Dungeon.

A city-centre-night-out-cool-dive, with a chilled vibe. A quid on the door for a stripe behind the bar. With weed and wiz on sale all round. Three bands on live and rooms for toasters and sound-systems.

They started on a Friday, then added Saturday, from once in a blue moon to twice a month.

The cops knew about it, but didn't care, there was less trouble than in the centre.

But the powers that be, the unseen powers that be, the drug barons and club owners, didn't like it one bit. So, they decided to do something about it.

One warm summer Friday night they sent the Outcasts, with a couple of Hell's Angels to supervise.

The place was heaving, bodies were sweating and grinding, bobbing and weaving.

Some African tunes with a flute lead in the one room, The Daffodil's chirpy-bursts of punky pop in the other. The place was rocking!

There we no bouncers on the door, just a

few people to take cash.

Out of the back of transits came the Outcasts, all denim and leather, greasy locks, and chains with razor blades in them, baseball bats and knuckle dusters.

They battered the guys at the entrance and waded into the crowd. Anyone and everyone was targeted. People's faces were slashed, heads bludgeoned with bottles, arms snapped with bats.

People panicked, they ran, they fought each other, they cowered in corners, they trampled on legs and arms as everyone tried to get out.

The Outcasts moved from room to room sweeping all up in a fury of swings, smacks and poundings.

Charlie and Lisa were at opposite ends of the Dungeon when it all kicked off.

Charlie got off quite lightly. Some smacks on the head with bottles, a few knife slashes on his arms as he frantically tried to make his way to Lisa.

When he found her she was lying on a pile of bricks, unconscious.

Lisa had been hit around the face with a bike chain; the blades had embedded into her checks, chin and forehead. She had also been hit with bats, her arm was twisted and the right leg black.

Charlie picked her up and carried her to an open doorway that led out to a walkway that lay above the cut. With the mayhem coming towards them he took Lisa in his arms, stepped onto the crumbling brick wall and jumped into the canal, and to safety.

The Hell's Angels moved slowly amongst the chaos, supervising. Stepping in when the Outcasts overstepped the mark, when the blows from bats continued after the blackout, when enough bones were cracked, when enough of a face had been sliced.

They came, they conquered, they left. They left streams of bodies in the street, fire engulfing the basement, and blooded, crying, frightened faces everywhere.

A fleet of ambulances arrived to take away scores. And friends dragged friends onto taxi floors, limped and dripped through night-bus doors, and hugged and wiped eyes, and comforted as they hobbled down the road, away from the cops.

No one talked to the police, what was the point? They knew who it was, but did nothing. Many were injured badly, scarred for life, the hospital was packed, no one had died, the Angels saw to that.

Everyone was shell-shocked, people's lives had been affected. People fought with less fire, people played with less passion.

Lisa was in hospital for a few weeks, she was badly concussed, and had her arm and leg set. Her facial and head wounds were deep, and over the next three months she had a couple of operations to try and cover up the gashes. The hospital did as good a job as they could, but she was left with scars, inside and out.

-You look fine, honestly.

-Don't fuck with me, Charlie, just tell me the truth.

-You hardly notice them, and in fact I think they make you look even more beautiful.

He stroked his hand along her cheek.

She snapped it away.

-Really, having fucking scars makes me beautiful? Go fuck yourself, Charlie!

-Fuck me, Lisa, what do you want me to say? I think that they don't make you look ugly, and they have done a good job patching you up.

-Patching me up, what am I, fucking Frankenstein or something?

-Look, you've finished the treatments now so we can get back to normal.

-What the fuck exactly is our normal, Charlie? Normal robbin', normal dealing? I can't go back to normal, Charlie, *we* can't go back to normal.

-Let's just get you the fuck out of here, and then we can see.

-Yeah, we'll see!

Charlie cooked her food to comfort and ease; corn beef hash, Irish stew, cottage pie, bread and butter pudding.

But Lisa couldn't find comfort and was uneasy.

-So, how are things in the big wide world?

-Quiet, everyone is still shaken up.

-And what about those fucking biker cunts?

-They haven't been around much, keeping to their own pub I suppose.

-I wanna hurt them, Charlie.

-I know you do.

-No, I mean I really fucking wanna hurt them!

-And how the fuck do you propose we do that?

-I'll come up with something.

-Shit!

The Green Man was known to house an old safe where the Outcasts kept cash and a stash, in the upstairs office.

Charlie was told that the safe was an old one, so Lisa favoured the drill.

The three-storey high pub stood on a corner, in a back street of bonding warehouses and needle alleys; of sooty grey brick, fenced off tat yards and done-up red courtyards which now hosted street food stalls and vintage markets, and housed hidden dance venues and gambling dens.

The pub held local metal gigs on the second floor, and the bar held leather-faced navies, leather-jacketed rockers and black dudes with spliffs on the go and blonde quaffed birds in tow.

They picked a Thursday night, they waited in the Carlou Café just down the road, next to the bus depot, with a clear view and sausage, tomato and brown sauce sandwiches, and dark stained mugs.

The pub crowds slowly emptied out; staggered or swaggered on home, arm in arm, cheek to cheek, in off-beat harmonies.

Charlie slurped his tea.

-Do you have to?

-What?

-That disgusting noise.

-Oh very sorry, your ladyship, I'm sure. Av-u-seen the state of your face?

Lisa licked under her mouth and lapped up the dribbling brown sauce, she proceeded to lick all around her mouth.

-Gone?

Charlie, sniggered, smiled and wiped the last smudge away.

-Class.

-So, the back door should be a doddle, and the door to the office.

-And you sure the drill will do the job?

-We can only find out.

At one-ish three Outcasts locked up the bar, and took off.

Charlie and Lisa waited twenty minutes, then paid, slipped a pack onto their backs and crossed slowly arm in arm. They passed some serious clubbers and hen party scrubbers, but the streets were fairly quiet.

Down the side of the pub is an alley, a

few bins, rubbish and crates lying around.
Charlie takes out his lump hammer and pad, and
smashes the weakest points of the door. It gives
way easily and with a crowbar he wedges it open
at the lock, they slip inside.

They both put headlamps on, squeeze
past bike parts, crates and piles of crisp boxes,
and tiptoe up the stairs. Charlie does the same
thing with the office door and they enter.

A desk and cabinets occupy one end of
the room, the middle a pool table, more crates
are stacked at the other end along with more
crisps and boxes of magazines, bike parts, a
serious sound system and racks
of albums. In between two cabinets is an old grey
Dudley-Chubb and Burton safe, four foot tall,
almost three foot wide and just as deep.

-Shit, this is bigger than I expected.

Lisa smiles and inspects.

-And gonna be a whole lot easier than I
had expected too.

She takes out her drill, magnified lenses
and tool kit. She drills close to the old
combination lock, Charlie in turn glances at Lisa
and at the street, from behind a grubby yellow
curtain.

Lisa stops drilling, puts the lenses on,
looks through the hole at the mechanism and

manipulates the teeth until they align. The teeth click, she leans back, removes the lenses, and turns the bar handle.

-Voila!

Charlie comes over and they both look inside.

-Shit, that was easy.

-What the fuck, Charlie!

-Shit man, they have tonnes of shit in here.

They start taking stuff out; kilo blocks of cannabis, full bags of trips, quarter bags of coke and wads of cash.

They leaf through the stuff on the table.

-Shit, how much do you think is here?

-A fuck of a lot, couple of hundred thou maybe, and so much gear!

-Charlie, we can't possibly take all this.

-Why the fuck not?

-It's too bulky for a start.

-No problem, I'll find some more bags.

-But we are gonna look suspicious.

-We can call John to meet us outside.

-We are gonna get fucked, Charlie, if they find out we took all this stuff.

-Doesn't matter if we take a little or a lot, if they find out we stole anything from them we are fucked so we may as well take it all.

-True, fuck it then.

Charlie goes out to look around for suitable bags.

Lisa starts taking the rest of the drugs and cash out and piling it onto the pool table. On a little shelf are some papers in folders, and receipts, and an old wooden cigar box.

Lisa takes the box out and sits down at the desk. Inside are some earrings; beautiful earrings, antique silver, with what looks like small purple diamond butterflies. There are other pieces of jewellery: necklaces, bracelets – of red and blue combinations.

A beautiful violet collection.

She positions the two earrings on the desk in front of the chair, scoops up the remainder into her shoulder bag, kneels down and continues to empty the safe.

At the door, a bleary-eyed Outcast watches her.

She turns, and they both stare at each other for a second, for a lifetime.

Then they both move.

Hitler Time at the Facebook Diner

I crossed the street through the rain and peered in, wiping the mist off the window to get a peek.

A bustling '50s diner.

I could see little wooden tables, set for two but all occupied by one.

I walked in.

No one turned to look; they were all busy typing away on little pop-up consoles.

I say typing but there was no sound as the keyboards were virtual, and floated.

The place was still a diner; waitresses dressed in '50s gear were bringing pie and shakes on huge trays above their heads.

Beers and shots were placed on little napkins next to the typists' hands.

I weaved my way to the bar, a huge wooden thing with cool flashing beer signs, and

climbed onto the high silver and red leather
stool.

'What can I get you?'

'Give me a Wild Turkey, hold the water,
and one cube of ice, and make it a large shot.'

'Sure.'

I took out my electric ciggy and inhaled
the vapour.

I slid out my android and found the
App.

The Facebook Reality Diner.

'That'll be seven dollars.'

'Seven dollars, shit!'

I fumbled in my pocket, counted out
some crumpled notes, and flung them on the
bar.

'Keep the change.'

'Yeah, thanks.'

One dollar wasn't much of a tip.

'You need any help there, mate?'

'Well, I'm logged into the App thingy and
just reading the rules and that, I think I've got it
but maybe you can give me the concise version?'

'Sure. Look, basically you go find yourself
a table, then you log into your Facebook page as
normal, turn on the App, and as well as seeing
your normal page you get to see what all the
people in here are posting. And you can see

everything and post anything. It's like an internal Facebook page and everyone on it is in here.'

'And I can comment and post whatever I want right?'

'Yeah.'

'But there's a difference, right?'

He grinned.

'And that is?'

'Well, if you don't like anything anyone has posted, anything at all, you can comment or, and this is the best part, or you can go over to their table and have a chat with them.'

'You say chat, but from what I can gather I am allowed to do anything, right?'

'Basically, yeah, once you sign up.'

'So, let me get this straight, everyone in here has agreed to this?'

'Damn right!'

'So, basically I can shout at them, call them all the names under the sun, and then I can slap them around a little?'

'You got it, brother!'

'No come back?'

'Only if they slap you right back.'

'And then what?'

'Well, then each "friend" has buttons in front of them, but unlike the original Facebook, there's a dislike button as well as a like button, and a fight button.'

'Yeah, I read that...what does that entail exactly?'

'Well... you... wanna refill?'

'At these prices? Shit yeah, hit me again.'

He poured a very large one this time, but charged no more.

'Cheers!'

'Cheers!'

'Where was I? The fight button. Well, if after a few slaps and you really can't come to an amicable agreement, or you just can't express yourself strongly enough in any other way, you press fight.'

'And I get to really fight the "friends"?'

'Yep.'

'Sounds great, tell me more.'

I took a long hit of the Wild and a huge inhale of vapour.

'Well, it's pretty simple, you press the button, and networking is suspended and anyone who wants can go with you and your friend and watch you fight it out.'

'What, like in a ring or something?'

'No, man, cooler than that. We have a room made out like a back alley of a low-life bar in LA.'

'Kinda like where Bukowski used to have

all them fights?'

'Exactly!'

'And anything goes, right?'

'Yeah, but no weapons and no killing.'

'But I can basically beat the shit out of them?'

'Yeah, man.'

'And no come-backs?'

'No come-backs.'

'Where do I sign up?'

'Just stick your card details on the App where you registered.'

'You know I registered?'

'Yeah, of course, we have face recognition cameras at the door; if your face hadn't been recognised you wouldn't be in here now.'

'No shit?'

'Big brother is watching, man.'

'Kind of comforting to be honest. Hey, pour me another of those Wild Birds and grab yourself one, too.'

'Don't mind if I do.'

One knew a good barman when one met one; felt like I had known the guy for years.

I sat down and logged on.

I spent a while browsing Facebook.

You know, the usual stuff; anti-government stuff, travelling pictures, cats, new and old music off YouTube, "share this if you don't like cancer", and more bleeding cats.

I read and "Liked" for a bit, then switched to the Diner page.

I could see what people were doing, the people sat around me.

I read, and then looked at the faces of the posters.

This was getting interesting.

After a while I started to really get into the posts.

Then I really got stuck in!

Philosophy on life, you know the kind of thing; the bloody Dalai Lama about harmony, or Bob Marley on woman, the usual crap.

Take that! Dislike!

Links to play games, shot down!

And then I got really into the comments, arguing with people.

Finally, I walked over to a woman.

'Look, just because I didn't like this stupid picture of a cat shaving a badger doesn't mean I like cancer, you moron!'

Slap!

She sniffled a bit and I went back to my table and Turkey; this was great!

A guy was posting to 4Square. Not only where he was, but also what he was eating and drinking!

I pushed the fight button. A bell rang out.

A leggy blonde came and led me to his table, you know the type, the kind that prance around a boxing ring in between rounds; big boobs underneath a tight white tee-shirt and little red shorts, right up her ars...sorry, I got distracted...anyway she led me by the tongue to the guy's table.

I sat.

'Why the hell would you post that, man?'

'Why not?'

'Why not? Are you for real? Cuss it's boring shite, man! Who cares what you are eating or drinking? It wouldn't be so bad if you were drinking anything interesting, like a rye, or a beer or even a fucking cocktail or something, but a de-caf latte! Who gives a shit?'

'Well, I th...'

Slap!

'Shut the fuck up, man! To hopefully make you stop posting crap like that again, I'm gonna take you into the alley and kick your de-caf arse!'

I had to Lol! I was taking him into the Bukowski alley, and here was me sounding more and more like old Henry! LMAO!

After I had finished with him, I went back

to my table, sank the last of my glass and decided to switch to beer; if I was gonna kick a few more arses tonight, I'd better stay fairly straight.

I slapped a few more people around, hey, even one woman – I'm no sexist! – for, you know, the usual rubbish about immigrants. When they started posting about Gypsies and Muslims I took them in the back and whipped their arse. Jesus, it felt good!

After a few hours, I logged off and went back to the bar. I was a bit tired and decided to stop the brawling and return to some proper drinking. It was expensive, but you can't put a price on good company.

'Hey, our man from Chinaski land, another Wild?'

'Sure.'

'You seem to be having a good time out there...I had a feeling this was the place for you.'

'This is just great, man, I mean I get to kick these idiots' arses, there's no hiding behind a screen in here.'

'Yeah, I was watching, you did some serious arse kicking back there...you used to go a few rounds, back in the day?'

'No, man, just read too many short stories, and drank far too much whiskey, and got my arse kicked in far too many real back alleys.

This is a push over. Suddenly, there was a wailing siren and flashing lights all around.

'Shit, man, what the hell's going on?'

'Oh, yeah...I think I forgot to mention this to you; I tend not to, else we would get all sorts of weirdoes in here, know what I mean?'

I didn't, and moved my glass quickly out the way as he untied his white apron strings and vaulted over the bar. He patted my shoulder.

'This is Hitler time!'

'What the fu...?'

'Don't worry, it's just someone has written the dreaded line, the one that all cowards and all people without intelligence use.'

'And that is?'

'You know, "What you're saying is what the Nazis were saying in 1938." You know, the longer a conversation goes on, the better the chances of someone mentioning Nazis or Hitler.'

'And?'

'And, now it's Hitler time! This time we all go out the back, and kick the shit out of whoever posted it.'

'No shit?'

'Yeah, you coming?'

'Wouldn't miss it for the world, man, lead on!'

Working with the Working Girls

I have nothing against prostitutes. In fact I like them a lot.

I don't like prostitution, or guys that use them.

And I really hate pimps.

The lowest of the lowest.

On the other hand, though; when I lived in Balsall Heath, it was kind of the norm.

Not for me, but many guys, friends of mine, to let their wives earn a bit of extra by turning a few tricks.

They were usually dealing a little bit, well a lot.

And I visited them often enough.

Would sit round their houses, having a spliff, and a beer, dinner even.

And they had nice places.

Steve, wife, kids, cat. A little flat, done out

nicely, top of the range stereo.

And Roger, been around since the 60s.

Roger had a big house, mock something or other.

Proper garden and patio windows.

His house was the house of your aunt.

A normal, go get 'em, working class family house.

And his wife would come in and share the usual niceties, and he would bid her farewell:

'See ya, Love, have a good day won't ya?'

And off she'd go.

Normal like.

But when I left, stoned, there she would be, on the street.

And she would wave and I'd wave back.

That's just the way things were.

That's how people survived.

An economy within one.

I myself lived in two bedsits.

Joined together by a long corridor with alleys off, to kitchens and bathrooms, and a cluttered conservatory at the end.

My girlfriend and I had lived in one, then moved on to two. But she left me for the guy upstairs who drank less, and went away.

Not sure how we came to get two, we must've come into a source of acquiring cash.

Not pimping though. Never pimping.

One day the Asian landlord, who thought he could be on to a good thing, introduced me to the new tenant that I now needed to share the bottom floor with.

Her name was Jan. About thirty, muscular, short brown hair, quite pretty.

But she also had the face of someone who had seen it all before.

She smiled with a kindness, but also a cautionary tightening of the crow's feet in the corners of those green eyes.

I soon learnt that Jan was on the game.

The street I lived in was in a poor area.

In fact, the crossroads was the meeting point for girls and punters.

And amongst the area of bedsits, pound shops, Al-halal butchers and second-hand furniture stores was a gentlemen's club.

By the garage, near the Crown, wedged in amongst the house sharers, surrounded by a hedged fence, to block the view.

There was always a steady flow of punters on that corner.

Rich and not so rich.

Both dangerous and seedy.

I started to get to know Jan.

And found her to be funny, articulate and

opinionated.

And I started to cook dinner for her. And we became closer.

Over time I was able to ask her the questions.

Things happened.

Jobs and boyfriends were lost.

Ends need to be met.

One time led to another.

She didn't have a pimp.

Was old enough and wise enough to get out of that trap.

But a big problem for her and the other girls was that they didn't live in the area. They had to take punters to their own places. In another poor area.

This had its dangers.

She had been knifed, abused, and raped.

A black eye was an easy gig.

That's why she had taken the place with me.

To be near the other girls.

Where they could look out for each other.

It was difficult to get places in the area.

Running a brothel carried a heavy fine.

So we chatted and generally got on with our lives.

And she told me two things which stick in my mind.

She told me that once you are in the life it's difficult to break out.

She would be lifted by the cops, charged, and once facing the judge, who she sometimes recognised, was ordered to pay a fine. A fine way above her legitimate means of getting money. So, she would hit the streets again to pay the fine for hitting the streets.

And so it goes on.

I also asked her if she ever enjoyed the sex.

And she said she sometimes did.

The city had two universities and many young shy inexperienced middle class kids would arrive, dispatched from greener, more innocent pastures.

To the land of learning, and opportunities, and pleasure.

In need of breaking that embarrassing duck they would seek out the ladies of the night.

And she liked that.

She felt like a teacher.

And she passed on secrets, secrets that she hoped someday may help the loves to come.

One night she introduced me to her friend Sue.

Same age and build, but blonde.

And they asked me if I would loan Sue my room for the night, to work from.

I saw no harm in it and disappeared for a few hours to the Fighting Cocks.

At the end of the night, they gave me a week's worth of government cheques.

This became a regular thing.

Me and my pal, Richy, who was staying for me, would disappear for a few hours to get stoned in the Bear, or sit with our pints in the Trafalgar, listening to the live blues.

Later, most nights, we would get some food together and cook for Jan and Sue.

Late into the morning, we would share wine and stories, singing and living the sweet life.

For us friends, sex never came up. Never.

There was always a gang of us sitting on those huge window ledges, speakers balanced, others on armchairs in the forecourts; sharing spliffs and wine; chatting and dancing.

Soon more working girls came to use our spot. A relief point between jobs. They sat and chilled for a while, shooting the breeze.

Our little hedged off corner became a security blanket too. Punters now had to park near us, walk on by us, or if a student, sneak on past and down the back alley trying to avoid their peers' contempt.

Soon the girls let us in on the secrets of the trade.

This inevitably led us into crime.

Jan and Sue, if they could, would relieve the half-cut customers of their heavily laden wallets. Not all, just enough not to be noticed, most of the time.

The gentlemen from their club would forget to lock their Mercs.

Richy and I rescued their contents.

The day's takings were thrown into the middle and divvied up.

That pot grew bigger!

Sat on that ledge I learnt and saw things.

One day I was chilling and passing the time of day. A car pulled up on the road past the drive. A guy beckoned the group of girls towards him.

The girls shouted with spite, and two-fingered this guy, sending him on his way sharpish.

I asked what was wrong with him. Violent?

No, he makes you take him to the countryside, somewhere secluded like. You have to tie him to a tree, with wire, and shove vegetables up his arse.

Good money, but...

I contemplated the whys?

What kind of veg?

Did some do it for him and others not?

Did he shop local?

Organic?

I chased him with my bag of sprouts and cabbages, but to no avail!

It was always sunny, at the beginning. Only later did it become damp and dark.

One such shiny day, I was sat, now in my usual armchair, just outside the ledge.

Passing the spliff around, chatting with a couple of girls. It was a quiet day.

We stopped to look across the road, to watch this truly beautiful woman, natural wavy blonde, dressed in a mink coat, stroll slowly down the pavement. Time stopped a little, we took time out from our day to just admire beauty.

And a man strode forcefully into our side view, heading towards this beauty and without a blink his fist connected with her face.

And the thud went through my jaw. And her blood ran down my lip. And as she tried to get up, he kicked her around that pavement.

My body moved. I had to save her. But the girls' arms held me, held back my need to help.

'If you go, tonight you'll be dead.'

I didn't go.

I watched.

The pimp at work.

Jan left.

She was moving to a new city. A new chance.

To stay with a friend. She had cash saved and the chance to start again. An inside job perhaps, maybe doing hair or make-up.

I was sad to see her go, but also happy, and threw her the best farewell-do I could.

We started to get asked to lend out rooms more and more, by more girls. Less older girls, less wiser girls, more desperate girls.

Richy and I smelt the cash.

We broke into the boarded up house next door. We furnished two rooms cheaply and sparsely. Black couch, one sheet beds, another sheet over the window.

We swept the dust as best we could.

It wasn't much, but it did the job. And the punters came.

It was seedy but people chose not to see.

A couple came, well dressed, nice looking, undamaged car.

Parked, went in together.

After a while the working girl came out to me, gave me money and instructions.

I was to purchase wine, pate and cheeses, and get together everything needed for a little soiree.

They were having an evening out. Her sitting on the grotty sofa, eating pate, sipping wine, watching her man pleasure another woman.

The situation started to get seedier. The younger girls lacked the class of those who came before. They were short on the sharing. They didn't stop for dinner. They started knocking desperately at our door, at all hours.

I went away for a week following a mate's band.

I returned to anarchy.

Richy had rented the whole house out next door.

Had furnished whole floors.

We were the runners of a cat house.

A busy and unruly house.

The cars lined the street. There were queues for the loos.

A few mornings after, I heard voices from out back, I sneaked a peak through the curtain from my bed and saw a group of people inspecting the old property next door, from the overgrown garden.

Vice Squad.

We closed down.

Went back to our simpler lives.

Now and then we took drinks and shared spliffs with the girls. Some of them.

But the corner was now a dangerous corner.

Pimps had moved in.

Along with violence and harder drugs, and darkness and rain.

I never saw Jan again.

That I hope is a good thing.

I hope she did alright for herself.

Hope she had never had to return to the life.

I hope she was happier, somehow.

And me, I never returned to working with the working girls.

Surfing Owen's Sofa

Joe walked slunk-low along the rows of fading grey-bricked buildings. He crouched but hustled fast to escape the rain and himself; to outrun the black shadows.

He buzzed the intercom.

'It's me Joe.'

The keys were lowered down in the basket.

He trudged up the cat piss stairway and let himself in.

Owen was laying in his usual position, stretched out on the old, green, threadbare corduroy sofa.

All his needs were at hand. Scales, rolling baccy and papers, needles, spoons, filters. Two remotes, one for the TV, one for the hi-fi, and of course plenty of snacks, drinks, and battered paperbacks.

Owen rarely left that sofa. His greasy hair had rubbed the green off the one arm rest.

'Take a hit?'

'No mate, I need to get well, know what I mean?'

'Shit man, look at the state of you, you need to lay off this stuff a little, you feel me?'

Owen had been on that sofa since the seventies, giving out his words of groover wisdom.

He dropped acid now and again, and of course puffed the blow 24/7.

He never touched the brown.

He wasn't a big moralist about it. He was a businessman, of sorts, and it was a free world after all, man!

'Go boil the kettle, man, and can you stir us up some pot noodles too? Could do with some substance me thinks.'

Joe knew the score. You had to kind of do the guy's general housewifery chores to get a score.

His customers would make him tea, a bowl of cornflakes, a few slices of toast, and of course instant noodles; the cornerstone of Owen's diet.

People would shop for him too. Take the list and the cash, lowered down, and then hoisted goods up in the basket to the hungry hermit.

When he had completely gone over he pissed in bottles and shat in bags, and waited until he could exit the sofa, just for a sec.

He loved that sofa.

He became the sofa.

Joe had gone on many a long bong trip with Owen, but on one particularly long trip he freaked.

He sat wide-eyed shit-scared as Owen passed over. Went into a trance-like state. Not hearing, not seeing; well, not nothing in this world.

Joe left sharpish and ignored the buzzing slow cars, and dangling whispering trees.

All the way back to his bedsit where he hid in his bed and chatted with ghosts.

Joe never went on a long trip again, a few blows, a couple of hits. That was it with the ganja.

He had asked Owen about the trance thing.

Owen told him that when he got so, so high, you had to fight your high, fighting from crossing over. It was scary shit. And you fought your fears, your heartbeat, fought your own demons, fought deep inside yourself.

But once you let go, once you passed over...well, the other side was a beautiful place, man!

Joe was fascinated but couldn't take the pain or the agony of that journey to the other side.

Half a journey had been terrifying, you talked with God and tried to stop your soul from leaving you. It was all a bit too Furry Freak Brothers for Joe.

Joe was sweating more and more, cold shivering sweats; sweats of panic and horrors of a different kind.

Horrors eating away inside yourself, like a thousand cold biting mosquitoes running through your veins. And your mind going a million ideas to the dozen; all shit, all 'what ifs' and 'sweet Jesuses'.

The kettle was boiled and the noodles had been stirred and left, perfect.

Owen gobbled down a few heaped mouthfuls.

He then set to work.

He took out his Bunsen burner and his top quality silver spoons and metal syringes, with sealed needles.

'How far you going, man?'

'Owen, I need a two mil just to feel myself, man, and then maybe another after to go up, we'll see how it goes, but it usually goes that way as you know.'

'Sure, but we're treading on thin ice here, man, were close to the edge here, and all it takes is a little flick of a kid's finger to tip you over, man.'

'Cook that shit up, man.'

'Sorry I had to ask you, man, but you know the score with the horse, I need to be sure.'

'No worries, man, and the readies are all there.'

He laid down his cash in the old Indian cigar box.

'Nice, sorry I had to ask, man. You OK to hit yourself or shall I do the honours?'

'You do the first one, man, I'll get the second.'

Joe took off his belt, wrapped it around the top of his arm and pulled it tight with his teeth.

While Joe smacked his arm and pumped his fist, Owen went through the ritual of cooking up, then he drew back the golden liquid through the little cotton bud, flicked the remaining air bubbles out and squirted out to the two mil point.

Joe knelt down before Owen.

'Shit man, you're looking a bit thin in the

old vein department there.'

Joe smacked his arm harder and pulled tighter with his teeth and pumped that fist faster.

Sweat was dribbling down his face.

'Fuck Owen, just get in there, man and dig around.'

'Easy brother, let's get it done right.'

Owen slapped the veins and took aim.

Joe was breathing deeply and fast and his leg was shaking.

He flinched a little as the prick went in.

Owen rummaged around, pushing in, coming back, trying to hit red.

Nothing.

'For fuck's sake, Owen, get it in there!'

Owen took careful aim this time, concentrating, and once under the skin he very carefully latched into a vein.

He drew back, and red entered the brown.

A beautiful sight.

'Fuck, let's go, Owen!'

'Cool man, just making sure, patience is the key.'

Owen pulled back a little more, more red; he slowly pushed.

Joe's head fell back as a warm wave of love, and care, and happiness ran through his body.

Joe nodded as his brain relaxed inside his skull, he leant to one side, and felt well.

'We cool, man?'

'We're toad-in-the-hole, Owen.'

Joe leaned forward, stopped himself nodding out, lit a fag, sat back and stretched, and chilled.

He let out a long puff of smoke.

'So, how's tricks with Mr Owen?'

'All's Cool and the Gang, man.'

Owen was getting a big bong set up.

'You should try a hit of this black, man, it's like a fine wine.'

'I'll have a little toot with ya, man.'

Owen got into his stride, performing like an artist. Joe loved watching him work.

All done, Owen lit up and took a long, long hit.

Joe smiled, lungs like balloons that guy.

He held it in for an age then let out a slow volcano.

Joe took a smaller hit.

'Hey Joe, I was watching that Coppola flick, you know *Rumble Fish*, the other night; and one dude said, "You ain't never fucked until you've fucked a wild woman on heroin." Any truth in that, man?'

Joe laughed.

Owen intrigued him. He lived in his own little world. He never went out. He lived through his interaction with his customers. He got most of his info off the TV, and books written in the 60s. He loved to give others the benefits of his bong philosophy.

He didn't have a life as normal people did, but seemed as happy as.

No worries, no cares, no stress. And he was never ill; sure, sometimes he was bummed out down, but never ill. That bong kept him healthy, content and sofaly wise!

'Owen, that's just films, man.'

'Yeah but a wild woman on heroin, the best fuck a man can get?'

'It's up there, Owen, it's up there.'

Owen never fucked, well as far as Joe knew he didn't. Maybe some working girl came round to visit him on the sofa. He certainly would never have gone out to meet any woman.

'OK, man, I'm ready to fly now, man!'

'You sure, man? Another two mil, dangerous ground, I told you.'

'Owen, all's well my man.'

'Fine, knock yourself out. Oh, and make us a cup of tea while you're boiling up would ya?'

Joe went through all the preparation, but this time was buzzing with the excitement of the needle too. His whole body was shaking, his mouth drying up. He sat back in the armchair, hit red and pushed...

'You OK there, brother?'

'I'm Sly and the Family Stone, Owen.'

Shorelines

And there I floated along the shores of Paris, vaulting the crumbling warehouses, tap-dancing over cobbled streets.

Passing lazy cats and blooming window boxes, outside faded little *boulangeries* squeezed in between high tenements. Shop fronts of spiralled perfume bottles and dangly copper earrings, second-hand scuffed suits and shined brogues. I climbed over yards with draped house boats, balanced along slim walkways, rocking on brown waters. Some high, some low, storeys of water, sewers and life, always life.

A small shop with pies, another bins of spice, an assortment of artichokes and beans, and hanging bunched herbs. And then a chocolate croissant bakery bellowing out a scent of heaven on earth from a chimney at a right-angle into an iron fire escape alley cat row. Little bells knocked by doors ring pleasure. Pleasure for the stevedore, the barge runner, the rag lady;

for the sellers of oily lamps, wardrobes, and
Chinese tar.

Pleasure and grit, pissoirs and spit.

I scrambled along a walkway of a blue
barge, watching my step. I was looking for a café,
it had existed twenty years or more ago. A little
red wooden thing, the type pictured on a
postcard. It was wedged in between the multi-
layered cobbles, under a bridge, up upon a
viaduct of garages for second hand Citroens,
table polishers and butchers. Safecrackers in
garage hideaways.

It was there. It hadn't changed much, a
little more flaky but that was about it. I walked
in. There she was, still blonde, still at her stool at
the end of the bar. I walked up, sat down next to
her and ordered a vin rouge and a strong
espresso. I lit a Marlboro, I couldn't stand those
French fags no matter how cool the box was.

So, we meet again.

What are you, Mickey Spillane?

What else should I say?

Hi, Mia, how the devil have you been?

Ah but Mia, I know the devil you have
been.

You my friend know nothing, and of that
nothing you know very little.

But Mia, I have climbed over wrecked

ships and fought through iron scrap to see you.

Cut the crap, Mickey, you got my note then? I wasn't sure after all this time.

Twenty years.

Is it so little? Doesn't time drag when life's a piece of shit?

Jesus, you got bitter as well as twisted. Let's have a few drinks and maybe catch a bite to eat in the Marais later, to catch up, twenty years sure is a lot of catching up time.

If it's not business Mickey, I ain't interested, and no one eats in the Marais anymore. Where've you been?

Away, for too long it seems…Is our bikers' bar still there, where we fell in love in leather, to Jim Morrison and Jack Daniels and smack. You know, on Rue de Lappe?

You always were the delusional romantic, Mickey, that dump changed way back, some drum and base cocktail shit hole now.

The religion and porno bistro?

Still there, but too trendy.

What about the magician's restaurant in St Paul?

Who the hell needs card tricks over a soufflé these days? No, my friend, the real Paris is around the 11th and 20th districts.

Oberkampf? That used to be a real blue-

collar shit hole.

Add a load of gutter chic bearded students and cheap good food in run-down buildings, and voila...you have your new underground Paris!

OK, another drink and then we'll head off, you know somewhere good to eat? It's been so long since I've eaten properly. I've been in Eastern Europe.

My god, how the hell did you survive? And I didn't like to say, but you have got fatter.

That'll do it for you. Transylvanian cuisine is the only thing worth writing to Paris Match *about, but even that is torture on a palate.*

OK, I have the perfect place for you, light bites of succulent delights.

Ah Mia, you always were a poet.

A poet, and a painter, and a discarded lover.

But of course.

We sat in the east district, close to the cemetery. She was right, this felt like the Paris of old. Crowds of students sat eating and drinking, mixing with beautiful things who waited on tables, everyone kissed, or laughed and argued with passion, and some read, and some took

notes and brushed back greasy fringes.

Over oysters and a sweet wine we
conversed:

So I got your letter.
I guessed as much.
A big favour to ask, you said.
*Not a big "After all the things I've done
for you Mickey" favour. I want you to
find a man for me.*
Does he want to be found, this guy?
Probably not.
*So what's he done? Why do you want to
find him?*
He stole something from me.
Go on.
My heart.
*What, you mean he stole your love and
ran away?*
No, he literally stole my heart.
What, like out of your chest?
Precisely!
Tricky.
Very tricky.
And you of course would like it back.
Well, yes, but just for appearances sake.
Could be distressing.
Why?
*Well, what do you think he has done with
it? In my experience the first few days are vital
when tracking a heart... You know, things have*

been done to them or they have been put to various uses. How long has he had yours, a week?

She nodded.

Difficult, I mean I could find it but it may not be in the best of condition.

But it's still mine.

Well, sentimentally yes, but it may not be the heart you remember.

I'm ready to take that risk, I am just not the same without it.

So, who's the guy and where can I find him?

No idea where he is, he like flew on the tip of a morning fog.

Nice, a name then, a description?

He is a son of a bitch, ugly mo...

Just details, Mia please.

Sorry, yes...Rebury, Tobias Rebury. Tall, skinny, good strong chiselled face, long swept back raven hair, wears black as you would expect and...

Wait a minute is that the Rebury of the back-alley duelling dens of Pigalle?

That's him.

Famed for his sword skill and lack of compassion; no opponent is ever spared?

Those duels of honour are played for real, the people know what they are getting into, or they should.

Agreed, but you want me to find him. And then what?

Well, kill him of course.

Of course.

But not before you get my heart off him, naturally.

Naturally...but the killing thing, might not be so easy, what with him being a terribly good fighter and all.

Mickey, you under-play yourself...I know you can handle him, what with all your years of experience.

Yes, well, I'm getting on a bit now, not so quick as I was, can't I just find him and negotiate to get the heart back?

I'd prefer if you killed him.

Well OK, I'll see what I can do. And by the way, my fee is the usual one.

You never change, Mickey.

She smiled, flicked her lace handkerchief at my nose and kissed my check.

It wasn't difficult to track him down, I just laced a few palms in the 'live' show foyers.

I sat across the street in an old Citroen, non-descript, me in a grey suit and sporting a long shadow. I smoked and ate candy bars and pissed back in bottles, after taking swigs of Jacks.

Usual predictable waiting game.

He arrived in the early hours, staggering and alone. He fumbled with his key. I went over and offered to help, and he thanked me, he walked up the stairs and I followed and helped him again when he got to the door.

As soon as he opened the door I punched him.

What the fu...

I turned him over quickly and took a gun from his pants, a knife from his sock.

What the...hell, do...you...

Shut the fuck up, Rebury, and get your arse in the living room.

I kicked him towards the couch.

Sit your arse on there...

So...you...know my name...Mr...?

He was panting and whipping the blood

from his lip I was trying not to pant.

Who I am is not important...You know how this goes down as well as I do...I ask you for something, you say you have no idea, I do you over a little bit, you tell me what I want or I shoot you, blah de blah...

So, you want to cut all that crap and get down to it.

Up to you, save us both a bit of grief though.

OK, what if I told you I have no idea why you are here an...

Shwap! I hit his jaw, his teeth crunched.

Now let's not go there...

OK, OK, the heart, yes?

He spat red bile onto the floor.

Yes.

I was gonna give it back, you know, I just thought I could kind of borrow it for a while, you know, put it to good use.

Borrow it? It's a bleeding heart.

I know, but she doesn't use it much!

Well, he was right there, but business is business, so they say.

It's in the drawer under the women's lace hankies and undies.

Nice.

I opened the case, opened my eyes and stepped back, just a little step...

I took a little Travolta drag, buttoned the case back up, turned and looked at Rebury. He was wiping the last of the blood from his nose and lips, he flicked his head back and puffed out his chest.

Now, why don't we settle this in the time honoured fashion?

I raised my head, then my arm, squinted one eye and popped a 9mm straight between his eyes. I had always been a good shot, and I sure as hell wasn't gonna give him a chance with a sword.

So, it's all yours.

I pushed the case along the bar and sipped my *Love in the Afternoon.*

Darling, how can I ever...

I held up my finger to her lips.

Babe, don't ask me that question, let's just settle on the agreed fee... How does it feel to be back with it?

Great, I can feel all these emotions whizzing around, dying to get out and back into me.

You want to watch that, don't let them run away with you, or without you in this case.

Droll Mickey, there'll always be a place in there for you, you know that, Mickey.

Mia, you and I both know there isn't any room but for yourself.

Too true, Mickey, until...

Until...

We brushed a brief breath between our lips. I turned, grabbed the other case, put on my overcoat, tilted my trilby and walked out the bar, and up the steps.

After a few flights I looked back and caught the silhouettes from the bar. A couple of would-be suitors were fighting over the lighting of her cigarette. She tossed her head back, gripped the holder's wrist and dragged.

24–7 Vikings

Bilson is a Viking town. Nowhere near the sea but in a valley. It was built on an old settlement, and the men are generally short and stocky, with un-kept hair and ginger stubble.

An old coal mining valley surrounded by the forests where Mr Hood and his band of ruffians had ran amok.

And not much has changed.

A Saturday walk up town involves a lot of ducking as bodies come through pub windows, and you have to check your chips and gravy for shards.

The place hasn't changed much from a time when the women of the village worked the lathes, drank like fish, fought like cats and called you duck.

The men worked hard in pits and laboured on sites and drank a half in each pub in town every weekend; up and down the hill of the

main road.

When barred from a pub the traditional response was to take a shit on a table to show your contempt. And after closing, there would often be a man or a woman standing on top of a bus shelter fighting off cops, half-naked, growling to the moon.

During the miners' strike there were no half measures...you scabbed – not giving a fuck, or you striked – not giving a fuck.

Three strikers got two years for blowing up blackleg trains.

And in the eighties, added into this concoction of volatile chemicals, was Speed, locally known as powder.

And the main man, amongst many about town, for buying, supplying, and evading the law, and being basically cool about the whole thing, was Squeaky Rob.

Now, where as other dealers and users ran amok around town making a nuisance of themselves, thieving and fighting and getting caught by the law, Rob was chilled out about the whole thing. He had other things to interest him, other things to occupy his mind.

He was a builder and a renovator, and he bought and did up old properties. But he was also a social animal, he loved nothing more than being friends with people, doing them favours, spending quality time, chatting whilst wasted.

Rob sold powder. But no one knew where he kept his stash, and that's what gave him respect. The unwritten law amongst the powder heads was, if you can find the other guys stash and steal it, then so be it. And the cops always caught people, with little bags on them.

But not Rob, he dealt large but never gave it large. He was dealing in kilos not bags, but the cops couldn't find his stash and neither could his customers or rival dealers.

So Rob had respect. Everyone liked Squeaky.

When he did up a new property he had a party and invited everyone, and the powder was shared around. No one went without and no one was asked to pay.

It was usually at these parties that you got to see why he was called Squeaky. He was usually on some powder but when the smoke went round Rob took a lot of totes, a lot...then suddenly he would start growling, and everyone would stop and watch. And his eyes got wider, and the tension in his jaw tighter, and his growls turned into squeaks as he went into a trance. For about half an hour. We would sit him down comfortably. He wouldn't speak but he squeaked. He was there but not there. Then after a while he would come back into his normal stoned state. When asked about this he said, 'It was the ultimate trip, man.'

Basically the high got so high that his brain would try to transfer him over to the other side, and he growled to fight it. And squeaked with pleasure once he had let go. We all wanted to know what the other side was like. Was there another side? Another side to what? Rob just said that after he gave in to the growls his brain came to life, into a collage of colours, shapes and imagined beautiful things; lovely things that made him squeak.

Now, around Bob there was a group, Aldo and the guys. These were a group of users, dealers, thieves, and hard men. The hardest and maddest of all the men who were down in that powder bubble.

They stole together, dealt together, got wrecked together and fought together. If they could steal from each other, then that was fine.

They stole from each other, but stood together.

Aldo was a little guy, a suede-head, and he lived in a caravan in his mum's garden. She couldn't have him in the house all the time, he would sell the furniture or rob the meters, but she still loved him, so kept him close.

Aldo was a hard man, but fair. Some gang had beat the shit out of an Asian friend of his, and he took a baseball bat around to the estate corner where the gang hung, and took them out, all of them. They needed a couple of ambulances to take the gang to the broken bone unit.

I was not from the town, I was visiting. I played with some guys in a local band, so I met these guys through other guys, and we met in pubs and on picket lines and also, when Rob needed some labourers, we all worked together.

I was invited to Aldo's caravan one night, me and Strinsky, a miner and occasional powder-head. And we hot-knifed black on silver knives placed on the little Calor heater Aldo had for warmth. And we knifed and knifed, drank scrumpy and listened to shit disco tunes. And I never growled or squeaked but my head went to another place, and when he played 'I Feel Love' I left and walked through a land I didn't know to find my friend's bed, where I chatted with a god, and waited for the morning, and the talking to stop.

I met Rob when Aldo, me and a few others were commissioned by him to demolish some outhouses in an old Victorian building Rob had bought. We worked hard all day and in the evening Rob came back, and around the room we sat on old dusty chairs and sofas and he paid us. He laid out old mirrors upon which, like a sushi chef, he carved out huge lines of white and pink powder. Each were given a mirror, some took a few lines, boiled up kettles, and plunged the gear straight into their veins. I was passed a mirror, and sniffed two huge lines up each nostril. I went to pass the mirror on...

'No, mate...that's yours.'

'What, all of it? Shit...'

Rob had work to do. He needed driving around, to various rendezvous. Aldo drove the van, I was in the back speeding me tits off. We dropped him off at a country residence and he told us to pick him up in an hour. There was a very quaint country inn nearby and we stormed in, and drank brandies and ports, and local ales, and talked to old men and danced with old ladies and had a gay old time. We picked up Rob, and he said he had things to attend to in town, and to meet up with him around 1am outside the local nightclub; there was only one.

We spent the next few hours flying around in the van, stopping and chatting to anyone we passed on the street and who we thought looked like they needed to be talked to. What about? I have no idea, everything and all things. Eventually, we made it to the club and there were a lot of people outside, and we mingled and mumbled and shouted and raved. There were some police there, and we chatted to them too, them knowing we were flying, and we even talked to them about that.

We found Rob, and we had a bit of banter again with some plain clothes cops, laughing our heads off. We got in the van and drove off. We were followed by an unmarked cop car, Rob knew who they were; he drove slowly, giggling to himself.

He took them 'all round the reeking', driving as slowly as possible. Then we drove to the cop shop, parked outside and waited for them.

The cops got out.

'Look fellas, I know you have been following me, I have no drugs in the van, you didn't see me pick up or drop off. Let's just have a laff about it and I'll buy you a pint later.'

The cops, were having none of it, they proceeded to strip down the van, searching behind panels, wheels off, carpets ripped up. We stood and watched, smoking, shaking our heads, grinning. We were then led into the shop to be processed.

'Will you fucking sit down!'

The Sarg behind the desk kept telling me.

'How can I sit down? I am so out of me fucking head I can't keep still.'

Bob and Ado watched and tittered.

'You son, in first...'

A couple of hefty looking geezers motioned me to follow them into a cell whilst they put on rubber gloves.

'Fellas, look I know you are looking for drugs and you are gonna have to look up my arse, but I have to warn you, before you do that, it's not a pretty sight.'

I'd had so much powder that I hadn't made it to the bogs quickly enough sometimes, and had

emptied myself into my keks. They, and
subsequently my arse, were covered in shite. I
was so high though that I didn't care.

'Heard it all before, now strip.'

'On your head be it.' I bent over and
grinned widely.

They inspected the clothes. Then I raised
first one cheek and then the other, as two pairs
of eyes and hands delved inside my shit-
stained arse.

After the others were done, and the van
put back together, we were let go. There was
nothing to charge us with...what could they
charge us with?

*"You are hereby charged that on the night
in question you talked a load of shit, and sped
around the place too fast and shat yourself."*

We went back to the building, had
breakfast and continued to demolish.

At this time I was only a sniffer. Most of
the boys were diggers. Hard core. Eventually I
tried it, and that was it. It was too good, too
much of a feeling of instant happiness, at
100mph granted, but sheer joy.

The cooking up was a rush in itself. The
anticipation of getting the power through that
filter into the syringe. The digging around for a
vein...whilst you tried to keep your leg still...the

hitting of red, the push...the rush...the warm pulsing energy.

And power done at such an intense level immediately hits your bowels and your balls. So after a hit, one usually had to hit the toilet. You needed to piss badly, and boy it stung, and hurt, but basically you orgasmed. You pissed...you came. The shitting was just par for the course.

So, I started to hang around the town more and more, staying with a good friend and his very nice quiet girlfriend and their pet mouse, and her fluffy animals. We played in the band, joined demos, and drank, and injected as much as possible. It seemed like every day was an adventure, and very often was.

I did bits of work for Rob, and he asked me one day if I had met Louis Light and Micki Zaveroli. I had not, but I had heard about them. They were legends, they were myths.

They were Vikings, and as hard as nails. They liked Rob, and even if they couldn't find his stash, and they tried all the time, they respected him and never used force of any kind.

And they looked different as fuck. Micki was over six-foot-six, massive bloke, Italian looking face, muscles in his spit. Louis had the typical Viking look going on, dirty curly blonde locks, stubble, short and stocky.

The only people they were afraid of were each other, so that was why they remained friends, to become enemies would just mean, well, death, literally.

I had heard that Micki had been one of the best karate fighters in the country, national champion like. Until he got into powder and went round the country and offered all the champions out for a full contact scrap, he kicked the shit out of them all.

Louis, I had heard, had moved to Crawly one time, to look for work. Crawly is a hard town, a Scottish town. I heard he was taken apart by a group of car workers one night in a club. An ambulance took him to hospital where he got himself patched, sewed and nose re-broken.

The next night he walked into that club, right into the middle and the whole place stopped and he flung back his mac to reveal a sawn off, and he sought out the guys who had attacked him, and a few who hadn't, and blew holes in their legs and arms and backs, and took the leader, kneeled him on the dance floor, and to the sound of 'Relax' put the gun in his mouth as the hard Scottish car worker, shit himself and cried. And Louis laffed, turned, helped himself to a drink, and bounced out of the club.

Rob said we were going round to Micki's gaff to do a bit of removal work, whatever that meant.

A council house on a nothing estate. Inside, two time-bombs. I sat, we had a few sniffs, a few puffs and sips. They started to story-tell, and my, how they could tell...

Louis egged Micki on.

'Go on, show 'im how good at kicking you are...'

Micki, to demonstrate, jumped from a standing position and put his foot through the ceiling.

'What about that?'

Shit.

They re-told tales of going in with shooters for Nottingham gangsters, to collect monies owed.

Of blow jobs for lorry drivers for tenners when down on their luck.

Of pierced willies, heroin, and finding dead friends.

After an hour or two of this we got some shit loaded into the back of the van, and we looked around for Micki.

'Where the fuck's he gone to?'

We looked at Louis.

'What time is it?'

'3 o'clock, why?'

'Ah, almost end of school time. Come and have a look.'

We popped our heads over the back fence to some fields.

'There he is, see him?'

And there...bounding through the fields was this huge hulk of a man. The full force of the powder and his desires rushing through his being. Arms pumping, legs bulging. A force of nature. Man and drugs working in perfect harmony.

'What the fuck do you mean, school-out time?'

'Fuck man, you know what the powder does to you, lust wise. Micki is off to wank in the bushes over the girls in uniforms.'

'You're kidding right?'

'Nope, straight up. Don't worry, he never touches 'em or anything. Well, not unless they want him to. Some of them go with him so he can wank off in a more comfortable derelict house or field or something. They seem to like the attention. It's just the powder, man.'

So, things went on like this for six months or so and things started to get worse, the powder started to take its toll. We felt ever drawn into a cycle of crazy ups and shitty downs. Our music and political output was stagnating. We needed to move on to live our lives, needed to leave people behind, to live. To have a chance to live.

The cops came for Louis one day, a Tuesday, he had never liked Tuesdays, and he fired a bow and arrow at them out of the window, they came back with an army. And locked him up.

The needlers got into smack and then started to steal from their mums and from their friends. And Aldo found Strinsky dead from an overdose in the caravan.

My mate's quiet, nice girlfriend left him for a one-eyed speed dealer. No more mice or fluffy toys, only needles and hopelessness and filth.

Rob got robbed. And got paranoid, and stopped squeaking.

We decided to leave, for a brighter city.

Micki's behaviour got crazier and he kept getting arrested. Like the time when the ice cream van came round the estate and he queued up, nice and normal
like, with the kids and the families, stark bollock naked. He casually ordered two blocks of ice cream, and lay on his little front garden with his erect nob in between the blocks. Tutti-frutti and a raspberry ripple, I believe.

People started to get worried, take notice. The cops were picking him up every other day.

They finally caught him. He pierced his nob and hung a chain through it, and around his neck. He then painted it with red nail varnish, and ran through the town, on a busy shopping day. A Thursday it was, market day. Up and down the hill, as was customary. But the fleet of cops chased him for a good few hours, over roof-tops, through factories. And it took a regiment to get that body into the mental home.

Time to exit. We had our bags on our backs and our guitars over our shoulders, and enquired as to the whereabouts of Squeaky and the boys. We were told they were in the forest of Sherwood, yeah the very one. And had been out there for two weeks solid. Just needles and bags, and not much else.

We found them down by the old quarry reservoir, resting on the banks, taking in a few rays. About ten of them. Ten Merry Men that were left. We told them we had come to say good bye. We hugged and patted backs.

'Fuck me, one last shoot before you shoot, has to be done like.'

'Yeah but where the fuck we gonna get some water to cook up with?'

'Fuck me, there's a big fuck off pond right behind ya, ya daft fucker.'

'I'm not shooting that dirty slimy shit into me.'

Rob stepped forward.

'Move out the fucking road.'

A different Rob, a meaner, pumped up cartoon version of the image he had been.

He emptied some powder straight into the syringe and drew back some mucky liquid. He gave it a good shake. And proceeded to inject it.

We all stood round waiting to see what would happen.

Rob looked up, went a bit green, let out a squeak, smiled and threw up.

'Fuck me!'

And the rest rushed to the shores to get their syringes filled.

'Fuck it! Give us some of that!'

They rushed past, laughing their heads off, shaking their glass two mils up with cloudy liquid.

And we turned around, walked to the station, and away.

Barman's Eyes

Corbierres was quiet, then again, it was never that lively on a Wednesday.

-You're gonna sleep with me.

-Dream on.

-I'm telling you... you're going to sleep with me.

-Just keep telling yourself that, but re...

-I know.

-Never gonna happen.

-We'll see.

She slipped from the bar stool and to the tune of 'I would go out tonight', squeezed through the tight tables, and as all eyes turned to watch for a second, she flicked her hair and exited.

-She's right.

-Bollocks, I'm gonna sleep with this woman; it's a sure gone thing.

-Wanna bet?

-Dave, you never bet.

-I do when the odds are this good.

-You're on. What we gonna bet?

-If you don't get to sleep with her, I want to see it.

-See it? What kinda bet is that? What do I get out of it?

-Sex!

-Yeah, from her but not you, unless...

-You get bragging rights. You get to say you bedded the most beautiful girl to walk into Corbierres, and remember, there have been some beauties.

-Well, there is that, but how about if you wipe that slate clean?

-And I get to see it?

-You get to see it.

-You're on.

-Fine, I'll have half a Stella and a cognac then.

Corbierres, the best bar in the world.

Bold statement indeed but true. Want to know why?

The stuff of legends in Manchester and further afield. A little light in a back alley of tall buildings, just a little light.

Down those steps into a cavern of characters, a labyrinth of rhythms, a den of intrigue. A bar stool for every story, every bum, be it slick leather-clad or worn worker's jeans.

Where snooker star sits next to Hollywood actress. Road constructor next to lawyer. Drug dealer next to bookshop manager.

All are welcome. All are found. No one sits alone in Corbierres, well, not for long.

That was part of the glory of Corbs. You could meet friends, but if you sat alone at the bar whoever sat next to you would talk. It was kind of the etiquette of the place.

The kind of bar that feels like a local to a stranger.

Women felt safe. Chatting up was commonplace but no slime-balling. Dave and the staff kept an eye on that sort of thing. And no one wanted to be barred.

Shit, you'd have to drink somewhere else, which was unthinkable.

Life without Corbierres was... Well, you may as well move to be honest.

Other things made Corbs the best bar in the world.

The juke box was an old one, an original, and Dave and a chosen few put the records on.

You had the Mondays skanking with the Isley Brothers. Public Enemy sleeping with the Clash. The Only Ones harmonizing with Roy Orbison.

A set list to die for, a sound that only old 45s make on a worn out needle, in a cellar that wound that sound around.

Always a backing track, never a vocalist. Ringing...bells for everything...tips, drinks and food...bells for announcements...bells for time. But what made Corbs the best bar in the world was the kitchen. Sounds weird when you say it; the kitchen. It added the sharpness to its edge.

Want a new telly and video? Pop into the kitchen.

Latest hard backs? Write your requirements down and pin it on the food orders board.

Message passed on down the line?

Whisper in Georgie's ear and the journey will begin.

Need information on a bust, a raid, a gig, a love affair; stick your head round. You'll get it served. In between burger and chips, a good burger, mind, and proper chips.

All will be fried up, wrapped in fat, served on a bed of goodwill and sent with tenderness.

Georgie brought the radio through.

'Listen up, guys.'

It was early evening going into night, 6.35 to you. The straight-from-work crowd were intermingling with the out-crowd. A time for sharing. A little snifter for the fading actor from the theatre upstairs, in between curtain calls.

The eighth lager for the cable labourers, who had finished in town at about 3.30.

The headline had been on a few times already.

The bar listened.

Police are investigating a robbery of a large consignment of jeans from a warehouse in Salford. Police said that as many as 10,000 pairs of Levi 501s were taken.

Glasses were raised as pants were admired.

Police say that they have no leads at the moment but ask for anyone with information to come forward.

Hooray! And laughter all round as, like a Mexican wave, black-clad denim bums were paraded.

If the police had walked in at that moment, they would have found fifty leads to go

on.

Corbierres was a community.

Summed up by the communal gatherings on a weekend.

After a casual staggered getting together on Saturday morning, the sharing of bruises and stories, conquests and embarrassments, a large gang ventured upstairs to drinking further afield.

One afternoon, The Steak and Ale House, a black and white pub where after consuming pies and black drinks, all who gathered launched into an impromptu rendition of 'Shake a tail feather' on the tables and chairs.

A community who took speed on a Sunday afternoon at the back of the Archway Club, opened up especially, with the sounds pounding around the canal basin.

Those who left the bar en masse to go to the trade union club to watch Man Utd lift the cup as winners, woke up to lost jobs, and waited in A and E wards with broken shoulders.

-Another?

-Well, go on then.

-You were saying...

-Yeah, I was a dancer for some years, then left 'cus of all the hassle and all the drinking.

-Cheers!

-Cheers.

-So, you ended up in Manchester.

-Yeah, after leaving my French husband, I didn't know what to do. So, a friend invited me to stay in her flat here.

-And you decided to stay on?

-Yeah, well, it's a cool town; good restaurants and theatre and bars, of course.

-And you found your way here?

-Yeah, felt like I belonged.

(See, Corbierres does that.)

-Happens to us all.

-Anyway, about this meal I've been promised.

-I have oak-smoked white wine chilling as we speak, and fresh Dublin bay prawns waiting to be sautéed off. A little salad and a Basque gateaux.

-And you have all this ready? And you are so sure I'm gonna say yes, now, at this moment?

-What woman can resist a meal cooked by a man?

-OK, fine, but let's get this straight here and now, for the final time. There's no way I'm gonna sleep with you.

-We'll see.

-Jesus H Christ, now look...let's just see how the night progresses, OK?

-Yeah, let's not spoil the moment with talk of sex.

-Exactly!

-What happens, happens.

-There you go ag...

-OK, OK, just kidding.

-So, how long have yo...

A little duck pate, little circles of French bread.

A melon diced on the side.

Peppers, onions and garlic fried up. The prawns soaked in olive oil and coriander leaves then whooshed onto the hot plate, slithers of garlic thrown on top, a sprinkling of chili too.

Right at the end, tossed with the peppers and a dash of wine, to steam.

Followed by a little leaf action; chicory, endives, rocket and walnuts, tossed with balsamic.

Gateaux and espresso.

Then continuing the smoked theme; a goat's cheese, cognac and Marlboro soft.

They chatted and flirted. Chatted and flirted.

He leant in and brushed her hair, and as the smoke left his lips, he brushed her cheek and the corner of her red lipstick.

-Well, Dave, set up those beers for one and all.

Cheers all round. The night crowd were in.

-And let's put it on the new tab.

-You're kidding?

-No, mate, like I told you, a sure done thing.

-Un-fucking-believable!

-I told ya, never fails.

-And you...you gonna see her again?

-Ah now, Dave, who can foretell the fortunes of love after the first shag.

-Un-fucking-believable!

Beers were placed on the bar, a row of ten.

-To women!

-Women!

-And to IT, may it remain unseen to a barman's eyes.

-Barman's eyes!

Escape

'Smradlava ciganka'
They circled round holding hands. Her head twitched back as faces snapped towards her own. She clutched her new satchel for comfort as chants were spat out. 'Smradlava ciganka.' Dirty gypsy, smelly liar; the two words mean the same in Czech slang.
In the morning she had looked proudly at herself in the cracked mirror, she twirled in her hand-sewn flowery dress, her second-hand red shoes shone as new. Her mother had lovingly braided her hair as she sang a sweet sad song.

Oh my love has gone, he drank and went to her arms, he lies now in her bed and I'm left only with empty bellies.

The new teacher came over and broke up the ring of poisoned posies. The woman's gingerbread red hair struck the girl, comforted her. She was dressed in trousers and a shawl, and spoke with a strange accent. Her face was pretty, speckled with freckles, angel kisses, her grandmother had told her. Her angel supported her over the playground and through the doors.

Now she was at the big school. She kept herself to herself as much as she could. They had all just been
little girls together at the small school; her friends had helped her catch up. Here it was difficult to make friends, she tried to blend in, but the taunts came day after day; she took to hiding in various places during break times.

The cleaning ladies had a little cupboard in the cellar. They invited her in. She sat silently nibbling a piece of over-sweet cake amidst the hanging smoke and the nose tingling smell that came from the rows of musty green bottles. The women pulled up their grey stockings and swigged and sipped tea and let fly with coarse stories of handsome farmhands in haystacks, drunken fumbles with party officials in stuffy file filled rooms.

'You ignore them, love, you don't take any notice of them.'

'But why are they so stupid?'

'They are all stuck up little rich bums, their fathers committed crimes to get where they are, you know?'

'I'm not so different from them am I?'

'You just work hard, my sweet little kitten.'

'I will, but it's hard when you feel afraid.'

'Their mothers slept their way up the ladder, you know?'

'Slept their way with the snakes you mean!'

Cackles all round.

'You're pretty enough, you'll find yourself a nice rich man.'

When the women weren't there she would go to her angel's classroom and quickly read the little books of Romany poetry the teacher had got especially for her.

When I have done hard work, I shall come and bring you money and happiness, because I love you. And you will kiss me, then I'll forget about you and marry another.

In her normal classes she worked hard and learnt very quickly, despite the old teachers putting her at the back and giving her bad marks for the *gulas* smudges in her exercise books.

'Where are your gym shoes, Erzika?'

'I'm sorry, Mam, I don't have any.'

When the class ran, she ran barefoot. Her new bright white Nikes remained in the box, hidden in her mum's wardrobe away from her father. Too many questions would be whispered at school.

The classes brought exciting new things to her. Gave her the chance to express herself, as she hadn't before. In her writing she could relay the stories told to her by the old women in black that sat all day on unsteady stools under the washing lines. In the flowing colours of her paintings she tried to capture the beauty of the seldom seen but often sang about countryside. *We were going a long way meeting Romas. Joy, joy Roma! We were going a long way to the camp and there we were working hard for only black coffee and a piece of bread.*

History and politics interested and puzzled her. She tried to put all the pieces of the jigsaws together, but in their teachings there seemed to be something missing. She worked hard at science and maths and the other boring subjects, everything might come in useful someday. But, her love came in her angel's language classes. They read of impossibly beautiful beaches, of greed motivated murder, of women in pursuit of fulfilment. They talked, talked about new and exciting things: art, films, love, politics. She loved it all! She was asked to give an opinion. She could express herself here like the other students, very often better. She sat at the front and learned.

'But these are traditional Romany songs and poems.'

'I know that, Miss, but you don't understand, I love to sing these songs and listen to the beautiful words of the poets, but I think what the words actually say is, well, a little bit stupid.'

'But it's important for you to have a sense of your heritage, of your own people's culture. You should celebrate the beauty of your history.'

'You don't think what they sing about is really crap, really bad for the women?'

'I think you have to look beyond what they are saying, these are all very old songs, with obviously very old fashioned ideas about relationships and a woman's place.'

'You've never been to where I live have you, Miss?'

'What's that got to do with anything? Now just get on with your exercises, if you want to get anywhere you've got to work hard you know!'

When Mum was shouting at the other screaming kids, she hid in the outside shed. When Dad came home drunk in the afternoon looking for a fight she hid in the kids playground nearby, ignoring the lurid slurs from the discarded boozers. Huddled under the cellar stairway she shielded her eyes from the sun peeping through the shadows of the walled yard. She marked the page. She was there. *Running down the beach. Her coal black hair shaken free, her bracletted feet squeezing the warm sand through her toes. The sweet green juice trickled down her chin. She watched the tanned taut bodies glistening as they struggled with the wooden boat. Their wide grins sparkling as they eyed her.*

But school was a smaller world.

'You fucking people are all fucking thieves.'

'I'm not a thief, did I ever steal from you? Why do you say such stupid things?'

'All fucking thieves and animals.'

'Have you seen the state of their shitty houses?'

'Yes, that's right, and you breed like fucking rabbits.'

'Have you had sex with your father yet?' Loud laughs all around.

'Why would you think that?' She would not cry, she would not!

'My mother told me, you all have to fuck all the men in the family, when you get to 14. It's tradition.'

'Yeah that's right, and my father says it's genetic, you have fucked-up genes.'

'Who told you such rubbish? Our genes are the same as yours, you idiots!'

'That's not true, you were thrown out of India or wherever you're from, 'cus you was thieves, that's what you lot have got, thief genes.'

'Yeah and they've got a laziness gene as well.'

They laughed their heads off at that one.

She sometimes slipped away for an afternoon in the park on the outside of the city, what a joy! Lying on the cool grass, watching the boats float by and licking a glamorous blue ice cream. She dozed.

The 15-holed black leather boot sent a laser shock of pain through her chin and up into parts of her head she hadn't felt before. She fell to one side. The picture went fuzzy. The red juice trickled down her chin.

'What do you wanna learn shit for anyway, what will you do with learning? Do you think they will welcome you into their fucking world? You see what kind of fucking welcome they have for you?'

Her father was angry with her. Angry that she was hurt. Angry he had had to shout at the nurses, that he had been made to feel the criminal when the police reluctantly interviewed him, scribbling haphazardly into their notebooks.

'The best thing is if we get you married off to someone who will look after you. Get you off my hands.

The best thing is for you to stay with your people. You'll need children soon. My father always said a little learning is a fucking dangerous thing for women. Don't fill your head with such things that don't concern you, Erzika.'

'She wants to have a good job, maybe become a teacher or something, to have a nice house, to hav...'

He let go of his anger through his nostrils and the flick of his arm; it ended in a hollow slap against her mother's cheek.

'Did I fucking ask you to speak, filling her head with dreams? That's what happens when women speak, they create shit all around them. Your place is next to a husband; your place is to bring children into this world.' That afternoon's Pivo was wearing off, and now he was waffling.

'We have to keep our people strong, we have to survive. We came close to losing it all once, now we are fighting again and maybe we'll not be so lucky next time.'

He walked out through the broken cooker-filled passageway, kicked a bony dog and joined other fat dark-skinned men at the kiosk on the corner. They all had their T-shirts rolled

up, proudly showing off their huge bellies; one
guy was singing a little ditty.

*Every evening I look at my window and
think of her mum, because I beat her.
Unfaithful, till I killed her. Now I have no choice
but to be jailed for two years. Mum, how
sorrowful the world.* Erzika stopped going to
school. She was in tears too often. Maybe her
father was right. She helped the women with the
chores. Scrubbed the clothes on the balcony.
Searched for vegetables from the closed market
floor. Grabbed her little brothers' ears and
kicked their scrawny arses home from the slot
machine bars.

She still listened to the songs from the big
breasted women who waited on the corner every
day smoking continuously, late in the afternoon
whilst the men were still in the bars.

*In the morning I went to the farmer's
fields, and picked his plums. I gave them to my
love when he left to look for work.*

But when she could, she liked to slip
away to the local library to lose herself for an
afternoon. Lose herself in the exciting new
books by young female writers.

*Joanna placed the picture back on the
fireplace. What had he left her with? She
searched the room. A few books and homemade
tapes, the odd trendy film poster, oh and*

yes...his favourite, the bloody huge candle. Nothing personal, romantic such as... She couldn't think of anything right now. No, just a candle. She picked it up and played with it, her mind drifting. She thought of his distant coldness that only warmed with caresses. His slightly shiny, slimy knobbly bits. His favourite colour red. His off-balanceness. His youth withering away. She recalled the nights of what he thought lustful passion. The sharp pain, slightly pleasurable, maybe even comforting. Shaking and gritting her teeth. The smell of gasoline, school classes mixed with perfume. Heavy puddles, pain like a niggling cut, soreness. She blew out the candle. No time to waste! She scraped the wax off her hand with a blade and straightened her long stockinged legs. The candle hadn't been such a bad present; all of him was there. She strapped the thin dagger to her calf, slipped on her black raincoat, turned off the lamp and slipped out of the door.

 Although her father wanted her wed, he didn't want to just hitch her to some waster. He tried to introduce her to some potential husbands but he also knew his own weaknesses and for selfish reasons he welcomed his daughter's willingness to get out and work. He knew too well many of the bitches who sat around the bars using their assets to get cash or drinks or a meal ticket off losers who had nothing, who would never amount to nothing! No, he was happy she contributed to the house. Had he been wrong about the schooling? Should he have encouraged her more? Had he just been too frightened, for her, for himself?

The Roma men were not that interested in her, well, they were at first, but after they only got a little, she always said too much.

'I would maybe like to go to night school, to study a little. I'd love to travel too, somewhere, anywhere. I would like a job; you know a proper job, something that I can put my mind to.'

'Oh yeah, yeah that's really great, but what about children and marriage, the things women really want?'

'What, like all the women round here you mean? Stuck around this bordello of an estate. Hundred bloody kids hanging off their fat arses. A husband who never works, drinks all day and then she gets a smack in the mouth for her pleasure? Is that what you are offering me?'

Love never really entered into it.

A man was watching her from the pavement opposite the snack bar. She had noticed him before. He was often sitting there himself, drinking a frothy coffee. He was about 25, always dressed in a nice suit but no tie. He

was slim, with a lovely wavy blond fringe he kept
flicking back as he read. She had been working
nearby helping a stallholder who sold cheap
plastic items, lighters, and batteries and under
the table cigarettes.

He came towards her

'Is this chair free?'

'I suppose it is.'

'May I?'

She shrugged her bare shoulders.

'I've seen you around here before.'

She leaned forward placing her hand
under her upturned chin.

'Is that right, it's not difficult, I've worked
for most of the businesses around here, you
know?' The lady-like accent was coupled with a
slight grin.

'Is that a fact? You're quite the
entrepreneur.'

'Entrepreneur is not the word I would
use, just a hard worker.'

'And do you know anything about
books?'

'Let me see, aren't they the funny little
things made of paper, god knows what people do
with them.'

'Funny! I'm serious, you see, I own a little
bookshop nearby, Bohomil's, do you know it?'

'A bookshop around here? Whereabouts? I know most places round here.'

'Ah, then you weren't paying close attention. Down Hasek Street there's a little evening school, next door is a café and bookshop.'

'I'm always too busy to notice such things.'

'Pity.'

'Why do you say so?'

'Well, you may have come into my shop and we may have, well, become friends.'

'Friends, I have enough of, thank you very much.'

'Look, if you are looking for work, it just so happens that I need someone to make the coffee and sandwiches, clear the tables, bits and bobs like that.'

'And you thought of me, I'm flattered.'

'You're quite the cocky one, aren't you?'

'And you're quite the charmer, with your offers of table wiping.'

'Sorry, it doesn't sound so glamorous does it? But it's a very pleasant place, lots of interesting people and we have poetry readings. I just thought erm...'

'You thought that with all my sophistication and style that I would be perfect for the place!'

He grinned, opened his arms and pronounced, 'Exactly!'

'Well if you put it like that and would like to buy me one of those chocolates with loads and loads of cream and sprinkled chocolate on top, what woman could refuse such an offer?'

It was wonderful. The work was very easy, just espresso making and serving slices of strudel. She read and read and talked and talked. The young poets with scarves and greasy hair fascinated her. Her dark skinned exotic beauty drew dreamers of exotic bohemian affairs. They loved to chat to her, loved her cockiness and flirting. The way she strutted around the tables, her dark hair hanging over her eyes, her naughty smile, the flick of her shoulders.

'Your poems are nice, very deep, but where is the romance and the hope and the adventure, you're far too gloomy, cheer up a bit.'

'How can I write about such stuff like that when I only see the struggle and pain of life?'

'The pain of life? What pain do you have in your life? The pain from all that Slivovica, that's all. Write about the beauty of life, the only struggle in your life is the struggle you have getting up in the morning.' The poets giggled. Their silent pouting companion's lips only moved slightly to a smile.

She moved into her boss's loft apartment. They ate strawberries in bed, went to the theatre and had weekends of walking and sex at his cottage in the mountains. She hung around the flat naked and cooked for him. They cried together watching black and white videos, drinking Moravian champagne. They discussed love and life and the hardship of her childhood.

She saw him talking to her one day, through a window in a restaurant by the concert hall. She was dressed elegantly in a summer dress and wore large dark glasses on her head. He was smelling her long flowing red hair and whispering and laughing and stroking her long fingers.

She stormed into the bookshop. In a corner was the young man who always wore granddad glasses and an old suit; he was reading Camus as usual. He was always looking at her but had never spoken. She walked up to him.

'Come with me.'

She grabbed his hand and led him up the back stairs singing an old song.

If my love doesn't come back then I will take another. And another, and another!

The Soldier's Fort

Up and round to the all-night shop again, this time a bigger bottle of vodka; too much trouble to keep going out.

Drink; feel better for an hour or two.

Food? No food.

Tablets; try these, maybe they will help. They don't.

Two, three hours pass; the booze wears off, the comfort of drunkenness wears off.

Different tablets don't help.

The pains in my belly are more stabbing.

The aches in my body more deeper.

Round to the shop again, this time Slivovice; maybe a change of drink will help.

It does; for an hour or two, then it wears off and the comedown kicks in.

Days go by. How many days?

People Skype. People message, people call. I don't answer them.

Can I get out of this? We'll try another drink, another load of pills.

I decide to cry for help; to message for help, to reach out.

Friends arrive eventually. Take the 50 or so empty bottles of vodka out to the trash. Clean me up as best they can; contact hospitals and drag my sorry arse and fucked up head onto a tram to the psychiatric hospital.

They see me, but won't take me; I'm too full of booze.

They send me to the Soldier's Fort, a place for cases like me.

Then I can come back tomorrow and they'll take me in. When all the alcohol is out.

A pleasant ride along the river in the ambulance; past the majestic monastery on the hill.

Through the ornamental gardens; through the archways, to park in front of the fountain and benches for people to relax on.

It seems nice. It all seems fine. I will be OK here; they will take care of me here. They will give me the drugs I need to fight the shakes and shivers and brain explosion.

They will inject me with hope, and dose me with comfort; all I need to get out of this bender, to get well. Armed police worried me, maybe someone was being difficult? Maybe someone was being violent? As I pass through the door the screams and shouts hit me; make me shudder with fear.

There are white-clothed nurses shouting and man-handling, and cops with sticks drawn up the back of some poor guy. They, as a gang, force the guy into a room, and there are more shouts, and screams, and the sounds of a struggle.

What the hell is this place?

Where the hell have they sent me? There must be some kind of mistake, surely?

I was questioned and searched and made to strip. I stood in front of doctors and nurses and cops, naked. I didn't care; I wasn't scared, I was just waiting for the feel-good drugs to be given me.

Do what you want with me till then. I understood most of the instructions; my Czech is not too bad, but to be honest I wasn't listening that hard. '*Yeah, yeah, yeah... get on with it, son!*'

Then the guy opened the heavy door to the room. There were two guys strapped down on beds, struggling and bawling.

'No thanks, I don't want to go in there, there's been some kind of mistake.'

The cops moved forward, the nurses pushed me and laughed.

No choice.

No mistake.

Shit.

I was shown the last of the beds; but not strapped down.

It was a beautiful room when looked at on your back; vaulted ceilings, historical arches.

There were three beds and a few more mattresses thrown on the floor; and in the corner a single toilet, no cubicle, no lid, just a toilet.

I was given a bottle of tap water and they locked the door.

'Will you shut the fuck up!'

The guy was getting to me; I eventually went over to him, and threatened to punch him if he didn't shut the fuck up.

I put my fist to his nose.

He got the message.

He was tied down.

I lay with a single sheet, no pillow. I lay and waited for the DTs to kick in, and waited for the drugs to help me cope. I lay, I waited, the DTs came; the drugs did not.

The panic, the shakes, the sweat came, the dread, the hell.

More people were thrown in.

We totalled eight in all.

All in various stages of fucked-up-ness.

Some old, some young. Some with blood on them, bruises, matted hair; all were skinny, all

were dressed in only the underpants they had
been left with. Some had quite nice pants on,
most did not. One had no pants but wore a huge
nappy; I didn't know why.

I could see the lice; I could see the sun-
baked skin that came from sleeping outside too
much. I could see the sags and scares, and gaps
where teeth used to be. One just slept, one
wasn't even awake when they chucked him in.
Some moaned, some complained. We all
hushed those who shouted; we needed quiet.

We lay and fought off nightmares, and
body jerks, and spasms, and shakes, and
creatures. We sweated and cried, and waited for
death, it felt near.
No drugs were given; no conversation, no
comfort, no cigarettes, no hope. Just water and
shouts when they came in.

'What's your fucking name?' They
screamed into the face of one poor guy as they
shook and slapped him.

He didn't know, he couldn't say.

Hour after hour it went on; stuck in a
cycle of your worst fears, awake, no place to go.

No sleep came to hide in.

Some managed to get to the toilet, to
puke, to piss, to shit; no one cared, how could
we?

There was nothing to hide; nowhere to hide, no need to hide.

At last it got lighter outside the caged windows; we could hear trains passing somewhere near.

Men started to wake, to sit up and try and get themselves together a bit.

The man remembered his name. Using slurred words, questions were asked, conversations begun.

'Where you from?'

'Prostejov.'

'How the hell did you end up in Olomouc?'

'No idea, I have no cash, no wallet, nothing.'

'I have no clothes, no cigarettes, nothing.'

'I have some cigarettes, we can have one together once we get out.'

'You know what I'm gonna have today? A lovely big cigar.'

'You know what I would love now? A nice coffee.'

'And a beer.'

'And maybe a little rum.'

'Oh yes, a little rum.'

They laughed. They chatted about their situations; how the hell they would get back to

wherever they came from; jump the train, take a
tram some way, tramp a long way.

They arranged to meet down the hill in a
hospoda; to smoke, and drink, if they could.
I just lay and listened, not able to join in, not
wanting to join in.

I wasn't going to drink, I was going to get
help. They let everyone out one at a time; taking
their time. With three guys left, I felt a wave of
terrible nausea hit my belly. I made the corner
toilet just in time to eject all the water I had
drunk that was now yellow acid. This happened
three times, I was the girl in *The Exorcist.*
I was the last but one to leave, the guy left behind
was still drunk; we had been tested, he still had
loads of alcohol in his blood, he was the most
damaged, the most blooded. Would they let him
out? I felt sorry to leave him.

I was given my clothes and belongings, I
went outside to smoke, and sat and shook, and
tried to control my hazy eyesight.

I got a nurse to call a taxi for me; I was
not offered an ambulance ride back. I waited on
a bench near the water feature, washed my face
and hands, the sun was bright and I tried to
avoid it.

I took a taxi to the psychiatric hospital
along the river.

I had to get him to stop quickly a few times; I opened the door and vomited more acid up. At the hospital, they tested me, they showed me to my room, with clean sheets, and pyjamas. They administered drugs, and did more tests and comforted me; and I had a nice roommate, in for the same thing; done a ten-day stretch so far, waiting to be transferred to another hospital for long term alcohol recovery.

I tried to eat but could not; only tea and drugs, a lot of drugs.

I read and lay in bed for four days, unable to move much, unable to eat at all, unable to sleep much; and endured the pains.

After four days I managed to eat a little; they gave me baby food, and I slept for longer, they gave me sleeping pills. I managed to cut off my beard growth of almost three weeks, and shower.

I walked into the TV room and managed to talk to people, and watch some Czech films, and even a little football.

The days following, I got a little stronger, and the DTs were under control, and sleep came in longer spells. I chatted to guys with problems with booze, with drugs. One suicide case and one schizophrenic; nice guys who spoke a bit of English, and we chatted about music and books and life.

I made some friends and gave money to guys to buy cigarettes, and waited for the drugs to help me recover, for my head to adjust itself.

And my wife came with my son, and I cried and they comforted me.

I convinced them I needed to go home after two weeks, I didn't need long term confinement, I needed my new flat, my son to play with, my wife to cook with, the town to occupy me.

Would I drink again?

Who knows?

But one thing is for sure, they will have to drag me fighting and screaming back for another night at the Soldier's Fort.

I Heard the Bang

I pushed my way from the plane and took a taxi to Long Street.

Big Mamma's bar was empty in the early afternoon, I sat on a high stool at the wooden bar and savoured a long one.

Si bounced in with a tan, shades and a wide grin.

We hugged, for a long time, we needed to.

'Too long, man.'

I kissed his check, whispered in his ear.

'Yeah, man.'

We let loose, dusted ourselves off, and wiped our eyes.

'Beer?'

We drank long.

It felt right, everything was alright again. The world was in its correct state again.

As if fifteen years had been a divergence, an interference between us being together, in this bar, with long ones on the go.

We caught up...

'So, why we in Cape Town?'

'I still have the old place here, I need to come here to do bits of business, but I've got a new beach place down the coast from Maputo.'

'And we're gonna drive all the way there? Fuck of a long way, man.'

'Yeah, but I know how much you love the travel, man. So I thought we'd have a bit of a road trip, Jack and Hunter style like.'

'You know I don't have a licence though, right?'

'Man, I am still using that fake one off that woman we knew in Lisbon, the one from London...'

'What happened to her?'

'No idea, you saw her last I think, on the rip down Smithfield Market, if I remember correctly?'

'Yeah, that's right I got wrecked with her for about five days, I fucked her friend too, lost touch after that.'

'There you go, so anyway – look, man, let's have one more then dump your bag over at mine, get a shower and shit then I've got a bit of business to take care of...'

'Oh yeah, what kinda business?'

'SA are playing a friendly tonight.'

'Who with?'

'Namibia.'

'We going?'

'No mate, it'll be shite but I am selling the beer and vuvuzelas.'

'Fucking vuvuzelas? You?'

'Who do you think introduced them here in the first place, man?'

I smiled. Of course, who else.

When we lived in Barcelona he had got me selling all sorts of crap; florescent necklaces at rock gigs. Photographs of tourist spots for tourists to remember, and home breathalysers, which weren't a big hit, the police never bothered to stop drunk drivers anyway.

We dumped and showered and hit the street. We scoured the stadium area looking for his boys. Si jumped out at various wheeled fridges and hawkers laden-down with vuvuzelas, and gave from the boot. Cash, goods and banter were exchanged. I leant on the window and smoked and watched the theatre, smiling.

'Wanna beer?'

'Sure.'

Si shouted, sometimes grabbing a guy round the throat muffling his hair in a rough but friendly way, and left the guys always with a smile.

A man in his element.

A night of the same and some stopovers for quick food, more drink, a quick dance.

We spent the next day nursing our hangovers; in the shopping mall for beers and juice, and coffee and full breakfasts. Then a lunch down at the waterfront; shellfish grilled, a white wine dry.

The sun-downing across the bay started off lightly, our hangovers growing into a feel-good buzz; few beers, couple of shots of tequila, some cocktails.

Between 6 and 7, bouncing again, feeling fine, banter and beers flying. The big Boers were crowded round the TV for rugby and made getting to the bar difficult what with their huge frames and presence blocking all exits and entrances.

We pushed and elbowed our way through. Simon stood next to this bear of a guy who had on a jacket of stitched together skins of various wild beasts.

'Did you buy that jacket or did you just fucking shoot it?'

There was a little delay, I coughed a screaming orgasm up my nose and splattered it on the floor, and then a huge hammer of a fist lifted Si off the floor and onto his back.

I jumped in late, laughing so much, I slapped one hand over Simon's mouth and tried to hold the guy back with the other.

'He's had enough, mate. Shit, he's out cold. I slapped Si around, killing myself laffin.

Anyway, the night carried on in much the same way, Simon naked on the bar of Mama's, me slapping some guy who wouldn't leave this chick alone.

We woke better than the day before and got our shit together for the long haul.

We stocked the Land Rover up with all sorts of shit; sleeping bags, tents, blow-up kayaks, cases of god knows what crap Simon was taking to god knows where, crates of beer, spirits, basic food stuffs and weed and pills.

'Why don't we just take a fucking plane, man?'

''Cus this is gonna be a wild trip of a lifetime, man. Half-way across Africa, by road, with Jack and Hunter.'

'Yeah, like on the road with arse-ache and jaw-ache.'

'Look man, I have some cool places lined up to visit on the way.'

'You mean drinking stopovers?'

'Well, yeah.'

'And a bit of business on the way?'

'Bit of business.'

He rubbed his hands, I huffed and grinned, it was gonna be an adventure.

Mile after mile of straight roads, and mountains in the distance, and bush and dust.

Little hovels of ramshackle villages, with black guys drinking outside the one store in town or just walking from one nothing happening day to another; from farms of work down dusty roads, to sit outside the store to drink to fill the emptiness.

We were not much better.

We drove, we drank, we chatted, we stopped, we gazed. We listened to classic tunes and sang, we sat in silence, and travelled.

We stopped every few hours or so for fuel for the car and us. Whatever they had going, in a blue tin shack with teapots but no tea, only dust.

We got *nsima* and a sauce of something green with a lump of gristle that may once have been attached to an animal.

We drove on into the light of the night that came down to push the sun.

We drove and smiled, and sang the words perfectly to 'Down In The Tube Station At Midnight' in harmony, into the African night.

Then the black came down and left glows in the distance and we drove towards them and passed on through.

We got our heads down as best we could, we picked up hikers on their way from farms to shacks in two-bit towns that sold alcohol, any alcohol.

We piled them up in the back and dropped them every couple of miles.

This was the nightlife of Africa. Crickets, darkness, staggering black guys on a dirt track. We put our foot down when the road was flat and mountains seemed a far way off.

Then...

'Fuck!'

Bang! Thud...smash, jerk, thwack, whack, fuck, p-panic, blood, bump, roll, glass...

'Fuck!'

'What the fuck!'

'Jesus fucking Christ! What the...'

Bang! Roll...body, adrenaline, panic, blackout, buzz, head, roll, noise, lights, body, blood...

Bang..!
Blackout
I heard the bang...I was alive
Out.

Staggering.
'Is he fucking dead?'
'I should fucking think so...'
'Fu...ck!'
I limped, Simon staggered, and held the blood coming from his head...I felt the bumps...I looked for bits missing.

The car lay in a ditch, front mashed up, arse in the air.

A black guy lay through the front window
Blood covered the splinters of glass.
The lights from the car flashed out a beacon search into the bush.

'Anything?'
'Nope, he's fucking dead.'
'Fuck!'
'Shit, man, are you OK?'
'Just cuts and bruises, feel a bit woozy, you?'
'Same, blacked-out but came round pretty quick.'

'Shit, man, did you not see the guy?'

'Course I didn't see the guy, I wouldn't have fucking hit him if I had would I?'

'Man, he just kind of leapt through the glass.'

We sat on the side of the road, chugging beer and rum to stop the shaking in our hands, smoking fag after spliff.

We called the cops. They arrived half an hour later.

Two burly Afrikaans cops got out of the car.

Large-arsed geezers with stupid wide grins.

'Beautiful night for it, fellas.'

He shone his torch around the scene.

'What the fuck have we got here then?'

We didn't speak.

They shone their torches at the figure through the glass.

'Well, you guys was fucking lucky there.'

We looked at each other.

Lucky?

'Whatdaya mean, lucky?'

They grinned at each other.

One beckoned us over and shone his torch at the corpse where the right hand was extended down by the dashboard.

'Yeah, lucky. The black bastard nearly got your mobile phone!'

He laughed, his partner doubled over and laughed his fat racist arse off too.

We didn't laugh. We just looked at each other, eyebrows raised high, looked at each other and shrugged.

Did he really just say that?

After a night of paperwork and more racist shit from the new progressive post-revolutionary police force, we were let go.

No charges, nothing but a warning.

'Your biggest worry, when driving in the Vild in this country? Not hitting animals, we shot most of them; hitting the old Kaffirs, coming back to the farm, pissed as farts, staggering in the road. Happens all the time.'

We spent a day drinking and nursing our bangs and bruises in shit bars in a dirty dead town, waiting for the motor to get fixed.

We got propositioned by hookers, but declined, we weren't in the mood. We just drank.

We booked into a droopy motel with a fan and a double bed, and after enough booze we managed to drop off.

We hit the road.

Miles left behind. Hangovers stretching on.

'Well, I feel like shit man. I think we should get some road behind us, then layover for a few days, somewhere chilled like.'

'Sounds good, know anywhere? Relaxing? And, I mean relaxing.

'Heidi's Hideaway. My mate Gav has a cool lodge, man, on the coast, remote, just past Durban. On the beach, good food too.'

'So, not a mad drinking place full of ex-pats?'

'No, no truckers or backpackers, but you know there's always a chance of a party or two.'

'So, we've just gotta hope for a quiet time.'

'Here's hoping.'

We drove all day, same old stuff. I mean it is beautiful and all that but you can get bored of anything. As night came we turned off the tarmac and onto dirt and sand, we had to get out a few times to dig our tyres out. We twisted and turned past mud huts and tin shacks, swerved chickens and chasing little kids.

Then, an oasis! A little bit of picture postcard Africa amongst the squalid reality.

Thatched cottages, lawns, toilet blocks, a huge restaurant, and bar with spears and shields on the walls. Dogs and ducks littered the lakeshore and a decking with an horizon, for dreams.

I met Gav, a mad Aussie pioneer, with a ponytail, a skinny tanned body, a cheeky smile, a drinking habit and a bed post full of notches.

A cool guy.

We drank slowly, chatted long, and didn't party hard, we relaxed and then parted as best friends to beds with springs and crisp sheets, to sleep soundly.

We spent the next day just chilling, drinking cold slow ones, eating all the healthy stuff on the menu, and lazed and let the world go by.

After three days we were ready for the off.

We were driving again.

'So, I'm gonna read *Fear and Loathing* and you're gonna read *On the Road.*'

'Do I have to?'

'One of us has to start with Jack!'

'But why do we have to read him at all?'

'Look, the two greatest 'road trip on drugs and booze books' ever written need to be read whilst taking a drug and drink filled road trip."

'But we don't have any serious drugs, and who the fuck cares anyway?'

'Jesus, you have no imagination, and the drugs will come, my friend; open your mind, brother and the drugs will come.'

'You talk a lot of shite, you know that?'

So, we each took turns in the back with each said book, with joints and cans, and every so often there would be a...

'Hey, listen to this bit,' or a, 'Fucking Kerouac man, he does my fucking head in...' kinda thing.

'I have to catch up with a guy down Mandela way.'

'Sure, bit of business?'

'Sure.'

'OK.'

So, we went down Mandela Bay way. A backpackers' gathering watering hole, full of Rastas selling dope, and dope-heads flogging dead horses. We hopped from one lodge to the next, full of cool over-land truck guys, wrecked by booze, and beautiful girls laid low from malaria and self-doubt.

Sex was on the menu at every lodge, along with burgers and shots.

Guys drinking their faces off, held court over impressionable beauties, who hung onto every tale, every adventure; every twisted tale and white lie.

Every lodge owner and truck driver was a hero.

They, and we, plied the girls with booze and tall ones, and took one or two to bed.

We snogged, we fought, we shouted, we danced, we stripped, we told tales, we fucked, we threw-up, we forgot.

We went to a lodge called Big Blue, and met Kev, he and Si did a bit of business out back. I wasn't interested in what, but cash was exchanged for small packages and larger ones from the boot.

We crowded round the bar on tall stools, and bantered. After a while he took us over to a table where three coloured girls were enjoying a jug of Margarita. After a little discussion a small trip was organised.

We piled into Kev's yellow Merc and hit the townships. We whizzed in and out of dim-lit alleys, labyrinths of seediness, and life. We stopped off at outside bars, where music blared out from tinny cassette players, and a few locals shook their booty. We snorted openly at the tables, no one minded. Some places were just a wooden shack, with a freezer full of beers, a couple of bottles of spirit on a shelf next to a lonely out of date football calendar.

We danced, we drove, we drank, we grinned widely.

The girls made us park up the car, and took us on a mini walkabout, through derelict buildings and flattened wasteland. In the middle of the rubble stood a once majestic building. It looked empty but once past the faded façade it came to life. It was bopping to gay dance music, reeking of poppers and sex and sweaty built up muscles.

We downed rum and Cokes and sniffed lines and little bottles with nice guys in the bogs. Then we all messed around on the dance floor.

A huge brick-shit-house-door of a guy towered in front of me and told me to dance with him. His torso was tightly squeezed into a country dancing flowery dress. His 12 o'clock shadow dimmed the lights, I hugged his thigh and danced. I caught a glimpse of a pistol tucked into a frilly garter on his other leg.

I hung onto his thigh and prayed.

After a week of braais on beaches, sex in sweaty huts in the middle of the ocean, nursing hangovers with slow food, sipping slow drinks, watching feel-good movies on sheets smelling of arses, we left.

After a week of bits of business at various stop offs we made it to the border. After a night spent with the Customs guys snorting Charlie, we entered Mozambique.

We hit Maputo running with more of the same shit. Supping and snorting with gyrating big-arsed black girls dripping fat from deep fried chicken as old men with Marlboro throats sang to a twang.

After three days of partying, we headed to the coast, our last chapters of the trip.

'So what you are saying is that Thompson was more real to life even though his is a work of fiction?'

'Yeah, for sure. Kerouac always bailed out, man. Always went home to his aunt for some TLC. That's why he's always philosophizing about bloody life so much. Too much time on his hands. Thompson was writing from experience. He lived it man, the good and the bad.'

I could smell the sea as we drove over a vast expanse of low bushes and trees and up and down dunes.

'That's it, over there.'

I could see a low ranch house, palm trees surrounding it, a couple of out-buildings around it, and then space; dunes and a little bush, and the sea.

'Beautiful place, man.'

'My saviour, my escape.'

'Anyone else living round here?'

'There's a couple of villages down the coast, not much to them really, just huts, a few bars. They have a football team though.'

'Yeah, any good?'

'Not bad. They play in the coast league. I sponsor them. Well, I buy them boots and pay for transport, it's mad really, the league. They compete for a big money prize, and spend money on playing when the fucking villages don't have toilets or clean water and the schools have no books. I put money into the school and try to help the villagers as much as I can, you know, buying pens, employing as many guys as I can on various projects, one way or another. Buy any shit off them, you know, putting money into the local economy, man!'

'Cool!'

His place was a lodge.

He had travellers visit. And you had to be a good traveller to get far off onto this un-beaten track. So visitors were few, but enough.

So, he settled into the life of being a Bwana. The big business deals replaced by little deals, for charcoal, or eggs or even a few lemons off some scraggy-arsed kids. Bartering with loggers, drinking with the football team, paying for breakfast for the local lawmen.

All deals were done on the selling log, you sat down on the log and waited.

Si would get to you eventually, when he had time. And he bartered with joy and a large grin.

He was up at dawn yapping with the night watchmen over pots of coffee, explaining to them how the world worked.

He beamed. He was flying.

All his being, all his life energy, if you like, was running at full throttle.

And after a few weeks I left him.

Alone, but alive.

Living but not losing.

He clearly lacked some companion, some partner to spend his time with. To share his love of living life.

He had sex if he needed it, but sometimes he needed someone to cuddle, and I could only offer a deep hug and a tear, as we separated at departures.

And as long as we can both still hear the bangs, I know we'll be alright.

About the Author

Nick Gerrard –

Originally from Birmingham but now living in Olomouc where he writes, teaches a little and in between looking after his son, Joe, edits and designs Jotte United Lit-zine.

Nick has been at one time or another a Chef, Activist, Union Organiser, Punk Rocker, Teacher, Traveller and Ecolodge owner in Malawi and Czech.

Nick has two other books published both available on –

Amazon –

Travelling for the hell of it. A kind of travel book.

Lyrics without music. Gritty poems.

His stories, poems and essays have appeared
in various magazines including –

Citizen for decent Literature, Bluehour
Magazine, Etherbooks, Minor Literature,
Roadside Fiction and Ether Books.

Contact and further information can be found @

https://www.facebook.com/NickGerrardwriter/